SHADOWS OF THE PAST

CECILIA DOMINIC

This book is dedicated to Patty Cheng: graduate school friend, clinical colleague, and someone whose laugh I will never forget. Even though you've been gone for a year, you continue to inspire me to embrace every day. I think Reine would've liked you.

COPYRIGHT

Shadows of the Past
© 2022 Cecilia Dominic

Ebook ISBN: 978-1-945074-70-7

Paperback ISBN: 978-1-945074-71-4

Editorial services provided by Evil Eye Editing

Cover design by Best Page Forward

1

REINE

The airplane wheels touching down woke me from a sound slumber and a dream of Lawrence. I started, hoping I hadn't been puckering up at the guy next to me. He'd seemed a nice enough sort, but as the hour had gotten later, and he'd drunk the free first-class booze, his attempts at conversation had turned flirtatious. If I'd given him a little assist to sleep with a minor spell, it had been for his protection, after all. And mine. My heightened strength as Queen of Faerie had allowed me to not pass out as I typically did inside the horrid flying metal tubes, but grogginess had crept over me the longer we were in the air, especially once we reached open water.

Sir Raleigh grumbled from the pet carrier at my feet, mostly for show. He'd spent most of the night under the blanket on my lap and had teleported into the carrier once I'd woken. That was another reason to make sure my seatmate didn't disturb me —he would have deplaned with a few fingers missing, and that would've been hard to explain to security.

"Just a few more minutes," I promised the grimalkin.

"He's been such a good kitty," the flight attendant cooed and used tongs to hand me a warm washcloth. "Can I get you something to sip on as we taxi to the gate?"

"No thank you." I wiped my face and hands with the warm cloth and tried not to grimace at the deadness of the water. What did they do to it? I sure as Hades didn't want to try any of their coffee or tea. Even a not-so-well-traveled Fae such as me knew better.

I sent a quick text to Lawrence and tried not to fidget. Oh, and I woke my seatmate.

"Wow," he said with a stretch, "I've not slept that well on a plane in a long time."

"Must've been that rum you were drinking. You'll have to keep that in mind for next time."

"Are you sure I can't buy you breakfast? My train to Newcastle isn't for another two hours."

"No, thanks." Newcastle... Lawrence had grown up there. The plane pulled into the gate before I could ask about my seatmate's business. Plus, I couldn't inquire whether any gargoyles remained and if so, were they related to my... boyfriend? Soul-bond mate?

Hades, did we even have a title? And why was I even thinking about it, considering the thing between us, whatever it was, was doomed? I had to return to Faerie to fulfill my duties as queen once I'd tied up all my loose ends in the Earth realm, and the atmosphere in Faerie burned gargoyles' lungs like Fae fire exposure.

Soon we deplaned, and I emerged into the hustle and bustle of the Edinburgh Airport. I toted the overnight bag Lawrence had given me and Sir Raleigh's carrier since I'd brought only my keys, phone, and wallet when I'd traveled to the US the last time. That was another reason to find a powerful Earth and Water elemental—they could make travel portals from one point on the planet to another.

My phone buzzed, and I glanced at it, then smiled when I

read Lawrence's message—*"Glad you're safely there. Hope all goes well with L & S."*

I'd confided that I had some trepidation about meeting up with Lonna and Selene since, well, I'd been a Fae bitch. They'd only been in contact because they needed me to help find their kidnapped partners.

I found the exit and emerged into the cool morning, chillier than The Aerie and Atlanta, which had been flirting with summer. I loved May in Scotland with its riot of flowers and continued chill, although sometimes a warm breeze teased the season to come. I pulled on my black faux leather jacket, and the lightening of the carrier preceded Sir Raleigh's appearance on my shoulder. I relished his familiar weight and musky cat-grimalkin scent as we both inhaled the fresh air stained by exhaust fumes.

"Mrrowl?"

I reached up to scratch him behind the ears. "Feels good to be home, doesn't it?" Although it felt less like home since I'd been to Faerie. Plus, my bond to Lawrence ached at the thousands of miles that separated us. I rubbed my chest and wished I could have convinced him to come with us, but he had responsibilities to a young woman who had just been orphaned. And that was partially my fault.

A sky-blue Mercedes driven by a chauffeur pulled up, and the back door opened to reveal Selene and Lonna. Selene wore a denim jacket that set off her red hair, and Lonna had pulled her long, dark curls into a messy bun. Her topaz eyes glinted at me with resignation, not welcome. However, Selene emerged, gave me a brief and thoroughly unexpected hug, and got in the front passenger seat. The driver helped me to stow the now-empty carrier and my bag in the trunk, and I scooted into the back seat.

"Good flight?" Lonna asked. Her worry for Max showed in the dark circles under her eyes and the thinness in her hands, which she continually folded and unfolded. Or perhaps part of that came from me being there, too.

"As good as possible, thank you."

Selene half-turned so she could make eye contact. "Did you sleep the whole time?"

"For a good part of it, yes. Thankfully I'm better able to tolerate flying now."

"Good. How'd the cat do?"

I gestured to Sir Raleigh, who had moved to my lap. "He pretty much spent the flight like this, but under a blanket."

The driver pulled on to the highway, and Selene turned around. "Thank you for picking me up," I finally remembered to say. "I'm wiped and wasn't looking forward to another flight or train ride."

Lonna extended her hand for the grimalkin to sniff, which he did. "Of course. We wanted to see you as soon as possible, and those would have introduced unnecessary delays."

"Has there been any news?" Since Lonna's husband Max and Selene's fiancé Gabriel, both friends of mine, had gone missing, there had been frustratingly little information. I glanced at the driver, who didn't seem to attend to the conversation. He didn't look familiar, and I thought I knew everyone in Lycan Village by sight. I could tell from his aura he was another werewolf, which made three of them in the car. And one Fae. And one grimalkin. Who would've ever thought such a combination would happen?

I blinked. My thoughts had wandered again, and I had to ask Lonna to repeat what she'd said.

"No news," she sighed. "Not even a ransom demand. Did you hear anything from your contacts at home before you left?"

I guessed she meant in Faerie, which indicated she and Selene didn't necessarily trust the werewolf driving the car with all their secrets. Or with mine, which I appreciated.

"No, no one's heard from Ellerin in the same time period, so that part of the story at least seems plausible." The original note had said that Ellerin had been taken, and the others would be soon.

Sir Raleigh huffed, and I could feel his frustration. While he had been sent to be my companion and guardian, Ellerin had been the one to summon him to do so, and so Sir Raleigh had some loyalty to the gray Fae, who also happened to be my father. I still wanted to know how all that had come about.

The honk of a horn and the roar of an engine alerted me to something coming up behind us. A black Mercedes going twice the speed of traffic wove between the other cars.

"Hold on, ladies." The driver tightened his grip on the wheel. I inhaled deeply and felt for any nearby ley lines or bodies of fresh water. Or caves. I could draw strength from any of them, as well as trees, although since those were living beings, I was reluctant to do so unless necessary.

"What is he doing?" Selene asked. "He doesn't seem to see where he's going."

Our driver pulled into the slow lane as the other car approached, still weaving. The whine of a siren followed them, so at least the police knew of the issue. Or was this a high-speed chase? Hades, I thought I'd left such nonsense behind me in the US.

We all held our breath as the black Mercedes pulled next to us and matched our speed. I exhaled with a whoosh and willed for them to keep going, but they didn't. In fact, they stayed beside us no matter what our driver did, and they crept closer like a predator playing with its prey. Sir Raleigh growled, and I ran a hand over his back.

"What do you sense?"

He didn't answer in so many words, but an impression of a thought came through, that the people in the other car had been looking for us. And now they wanted to hurt us.

The black Mercedes jerked to the side and hit us so hard

my internal organs sloshed against my ribs. The sound exploded through the car, and our driver slammed on the brakes, jolting me and leaving me nauseated and shaking. The Mercedes must have anticipated our driver's response because they did the same and slammed into us again. Our car scraped the guard rail, and I'm pretty sure we all screamed. One more hit, and the driver's side window shattered. This time there was no guard rail, just empty air.

2

REINE

For the first time since she died, my grandmother's voice came into my mind with calm clarity. *"A Fae queen does not panic. She looks for the resources she has and uses them to her best advantages, even if they are not ideal."* I didn't question whether my own memory of long-ago advice had kicked in or if my imminent death opened some sort of channel. No time to think about it. I drew what I could from a pond and the nearby river and imagined holding the car straight in its flight so we wouldn't flip. I also pushed to angle it toward an open field instead of the patch of forest beside and under us.

I couldn't do this alone. At least I'd learned that lesson in The Aerie.

I chanted in Celtic under my breath, summoning whatever air elementals may be nearby. The descent of the car slowed between their efforts and mine, and we landed with a thud in the field, which had just been plowed. With manure. The wheels landed in the foul-smelling stuff hard enough to jar us and activate all the air bags.

The silence that spread through the car thickened my tongue, and I waited for my heart to slow.

Selene was the first to speak. "What. The hell. Was that?"

"Is anyone seriously hurt?" I placed a hand on my chest and healed the seatbelt bruise. I also touched my thighs to close the gashes from where Sir Raleigh's claws had dug into me during our descent, and where they had ripped free with the rebound force of our landing. Then he'd disappeared. I hoped his absence didn't mean he'd been injured.

Lonna and Selene said no, but the driver didn't respond.

"Gavin?" Lonna winced as she reached down to unbuckle her seatbelt.

"Let me heal you," I said, but she waved my hand away.

"There are more important things now." She opened the door, and the acrid odor of the field's fertilizer wafted in. I wanted to dampen my sense of smell, but I didn't want to burn any more energy than I needed to.

A couple of nearby sources, the River Nairn and the ancient cairns, called to me more strongly than any of the places in the States had. Familiarity or something else?

Lonna staggered around the car, steadying herself with one hand, although I couldn't tell whether that was due to the soft ground or the injuries she wouldn't let me tend. Her blood sang a discordant song. Selene, meanwhile, was silent, and I worried she had gone into shock.

Once Lonna made it past my seat, I opened the door. Thankfully I landed in a patch that had a higher dirt to crap ratio.

"Gavin?" Lonna whispered.

The driver groaned. I planned to check on him next, but I stepped around the car to the eerily quiet Selene. She sat with her fists clenched, and I placed a hand on her shoulder. "Selene? Are you okay? Speak to me, hon."

She blinked. "Hon?' How much time did you spend in Georgia, again?"

Relief made me smile. "Long enough. Can you move?"

She accepted my help with her minor wounds, but she declined to allow me to touch her head to help with her shock. "I can take care of that myself, thanks."

Meanwhile, Lonna had her phone out and was talking to someone. "Yes, he has a heartbeat. Yes, I think he's injured. Please send help as fast as you can."

A flash of light made me glance back up toward the highway. A large black SUV had stopped, and men in dark clothing —black sweaters, jeans, and hiking boots—were making their way down the bank. I tapped Lonna's shoulder and directed her attention to them.

"Is that them?" she asked whoever she was talking to. "No? You just now dispatched someone?"

My pulse picked up, and the base of my skull tingled. "Lonna? Selene? I don't think they're here to help."

Gavin heaved himself out of the car and pulled a gun from his shoulder holster. "You three go. I'll hold them."

The way his aura flickered made me doubt he could. "You're hurt. Let me help."

Sunlight flashed on the barrel of the weapon one of the men aimed at us, and a shot cracked the air.

"There's no time. Go!" Gavin yelled.

Another shot and a wave of hostility emanating from the attackers forced me to teleport a short distance.

When my feet caught the ground, I sprinted toward the woods. Two heavily breathing people tailed me. From what I could sense of their auras, Selene and Lonna had decided to follow. Should I have deferred to Lonna's leadership since she was technically the highest-ranking of us outside of Faerie? Perhaps, but self-preservation wins every time, at least for me.

We made it to the woods, and the gloom swallowed us in cool shade.

"Are they gone?" Selene asked.

I stopped and placed a hand on a nearby tree trunk. It

rattled its leaves in excitement, and I smiled. With its permission, I borrowed its perspective to look back toward our crash site in the field, and I couldn't see any non-vegetal shapes moving toward us. They all seemed to be clustered around the vehicle. I thanked the tree, and it knocked two branches together to acknowledge my gratitude.

"What was that?" Selene's eyes had gone even wider, if possible.

"The tree saying 'you're welcome' when I thanked it for letting me see through it."

"You can do that?" Lonna's eyebrows headed toward her hairline.

"Yes, now that I've had my promotion." Fae queens have to be military leaders as well as political rulers, so we need to use nature for tactical and strategic purposes. I didn't tell them, though. Did they even know I was the new queen? Probably, since Lawrence had talked to Max and Gabriel when he was in the ILR hospital, but neither of them had congratulated me.

"We should keep moving," Lonna suggested. "If they went through all that effort to knock us off the road, they'll be coming for us."

I didn't argue. The woods felt familiar, although I hadn't been to this section in a long time. If I were to be honest with myself, I'd been avoiding this forest and its associated painful memories. We were very close to the Culloden battle site, the site of Rhys' and my exile. In fact, we'd sought help from a witch that lived around this area long before much of the woods had been cut down for farms.

I tried not to be hurt that neither Lonna nor Selene had said anything in response to my promotion comment. Did they not care? Or was I reaping the reward for having been such a pain in the derriere to both in our previous work together?

I stumbled, and Selene caught me. Although the forest was loaning me its strength, I had just had an exhausting flight and done a major magical feat in keeping us from crashing too hard. Which neither of my companions had thanked me for. The thought of smiting them crossed my mind, but I refrained from allowing that temptation any more mental energy.

"You must be exhausted," Selene murmured.

I recalled her empathic ability. "More than a little."

"What did you do...back there?" She flipped her hand back toward where we had just come from. "I felt magic happening."

"I slowed our descent with the help of some air elementals and kept the car straight with my own power." I tripped over my own feet again. "And I don't know how much longer I can go without recharging. A long nap would do it, but contact with the earth, like visiting the caves underneath here, would be faster."

Lonna and Selene exchanged worried glances. "We don't know this area that well," Lonna explained. "Can you find something and tell us how to get you there?"

We came to a clearing that at first seemed to be empty. I stopped short, recognizing the spell.

Selene said, "You know this place." It wasn't a question. "And something about it frightens you."

"Yes, but unfortunately, it's our best hiding place. I can unlock the security invisibility spell since I helped the witch set it the first time."

Why did we have to end up here? This wasn't at all where I wanted to be, but I couldn't think of another solution. I looked around once more for Sir Raleigh, but the shadows remained still, and his green eyes didn't shine forth from the branches. He could move between realms, I reminded myself. He'd find me. Meanwhile, I had these two to take care of.

"Keep walking forward and hold my hands." They each took one of my hands in theirs. Selene's cold, Lonna's almost feverish. I wasn't the only one still shaken from the accident, and I would have studied the two women's very different reactions had I not needed to concentrate on making a crack to slip through so I could find help for all of us—a good intention.

We walked forward slowly, and a tinkling sound tickled my ears—wind chimes. Another step brought a change in temperature from balmy late spring to chilly early spring, and finally, when we got within ten feet of it, the witch's house appeared.

3

LAWRENCE

I sipped my coffee and gazed at the back yard. My inner gargoyle, who had been integrated with me except for when I denied my emotions, growled. He wanted me to throw my phone across my screened-in balcony in frustration. All right, *I* wanted to throw the phone, and the growl came from *my* throat. I indulged myself in a moment of "it's not fair" before taking a few deep breaths of the late spring air. It already hinted at the humidity to come. We'd gotten beyond pollen season in Atlanta, which left us a few nice weeks of not-too-warm-or-muggy weather before the wet blanket of summer descended.

I looked again at the text from Reine and my reply. Only a short conversation, but at least we could stay in touch through electronic means. I caught myself rubbing my chest, where I pictured the anchor of the stretched bond between us, taut and sore. She was my bond-mate. I was hers. I should be by her side, but I had responsibilities. The main one had left her books, sweater, and shoes strewn around the porch the night before. Yes, I wanted to clean up after her. Yes, I knew it wasn't my job. And yes, I wished every day that her parents were here to do *their* job, but they'd gotten themselves killed in moments of foolishness.

Another unfair thought born of the anger that comes with grief. It was easier to be angry at dead people than at myself for failing to do what I needed to protect my friends from themselves. I growled again, this time at my own failure. Kestrel's mother had been doing what she thought was best for her daughter, even though it had backfired in the worst possible way. As for her father... John had suspected Kestrel hadn't been his, and he'd been goaded into his final, fatal moment.

Did I blame him? No, there was only so much one heart could take.

As for Kestrel's biological father... I would have wished for him to come and take up his responsibility, but no, he had Fae things to do.

I sighed and rubbed my eyes. I had a couple of hours until Kestrel got up so I could enjoy the peace of the back yard, the squirrels chattering at each other, the birds flitting from tree to tree, the door to the house opening...

So much for my quiet hours. I turned around and put on the same pleasant expression I'd assumed since Kestrel asked to stay with me. Of course I welcomed her. She was my goddaughter, her parents my best friends. I couldn't say no, especially since she couldn't stand to be in the house where they'd all lived. Still, I had to acknowledge she wasn't the roommate I'd been hoping for.

"Good morning, sunshine," I said, nodding to the cup of coffee she held in one hand. She had her laptop tucked under her other arm and still wore her light blue pajamas under a flannel robe. "You're up early."

"And you look like crap. Did you sleep at all?"

I patted the cushion next to me on the glider. "Not very well." I rubbed my chest again. I'd felt the ache as soon as Reine's plane had taken off. It was supposed to have left at 9:00

p.m., but it had been delayed several hours due to a freak storm on the south side of town right over the airport. Had her own reluctance to leave me caused it? Did I dare hope I had that sort of influence on her? Complications and ego made for strange competitors.

She plopped on the glider next to me, which made it swing to and fro. "Registration for the fall opens at noon, and I want to jump on my classes so I get what I want." She spoke in the flat tone that betrayed too little sleep and too much effort to care.

I stilled the glider. My stomach couldn't handle the motion. Both to distract myself and to make sure she knew she had my undivided attention, I asked, "What have you picked out? And you're sure you don't want to go back to PBI Academy?"

She wrinkled her nose and shook her head, and I caught my breath at her resemblance to her mother. The pain around my heart intensified as guilt and sorrow rushed back in.

"I most definitely don't want to go back to Paranormal Betrayal and Investigations." The *B* actually stood for Bureau, our kind's version of the more well-known Federal Bureau of Investigations.

"Right, because of Corey." Another point of confusion. What was my role with Kestrel's not-so-secret boyfriend? Should I beat him up? Threaten him a little? Leave the situation alone?

"Please stop bringing him up, Uncle Lawrence." She wiped the back of her sleeve across her right eye. "I can't forgive him, not now. Not yet."

"Even though he came to the funeral."

"Just because he came doesn't mean that makes up for him not telling me he was investigating Mom. That he was using me to get closer to her."

I didn't know that was exactly how things had gone, but she hadn't shared how she'd found out the information. Since she wouldn't respond to requests for clarification, I let it drop. I wouldn't lie to her and say I didn't think that was the case. I didn't know Corey that well, and cat shifters could be damn deep and inscrutable.

"Plus, he left right after," she added with a sigh. "And he hasn't tried to call or text or anything."

I suspected Corey's neglect had been the bigger sin in her eyes. Personally, I thought it was smart of him to leave her alone for a while. Their age difference of almost a decade had been a big issue for her parents, and the fact that he could potentially be her field supervisor someday had concerned everyone else. But Kestrel had fallen for him hard, and he'd seemed to reciprocate her feelings.

Who was I to criticize impossible or un-approved-of love? Here I was in love with a Fae queen who ruled over a realm that would kill me should I enter it again. I'd almost died after being there the first time, and it had required the care of a specialist in paranormal medicine to heal me by forcing me to integrate with my inner gargoyle. I only had the one, so I didn't think I'd be able to survive another trip to Faerie.

Did we do the Hades and Persephone thing and have Reine split her time? We hadn't talked about it. Neither of us wanted to face the possibility of no good solutions.

Kestrel opened her laptop and pulled up the school's online catalog.

"Have you talked to Admissions yet? You said you were having a hard time getting through."

She nodded. "I finally got to speak to someone late yesterday afternoon after you'd taken your friend to the airport." Kestrel still held a grudge against Reine for not allowing her to use necromancy powers to save her adopted father. Another thing I didn't have a clear picture of the consequences of, but when Reine had explained it to me, it had sounded like it would have been torture for John.

"And…?"

"Most of my core math and science should transfer along with the basic psychology courses, but I'll need to catch up on history and other humanities." She wrinkled her nose again when she said, 'humanities.'

"If you're going to live among them and pretend to be one, you shouldn't disdain them." She gave me an exasperated look, so I continued, "It's something we all had to learn, kid." Never mind that I'd learned that lesson the hard way when my mother and I had had to live among the humans to hide from the band of murderous Fae that had killed my father. In my low moments, I recalled punching my father's killer in the face and the satisfying crunch of bone. I would have broken his nose had he not been a quick-healing Fae. I tried not to indulge my violent gargoyle tendencies, but sometimes they happened.

"But look, there's this professor who teaches classes on local folklore. It would be fun to learn about how the humans see us outside of fiction and popular media. Not that I mind me some Loki. Tom Hiddleston is a hottie."

And not her usual type. Corey had the stocky build of a lion, not the lithe frame of the British actor so many women swooned over. Maybe she was still figuring out her type. I didn't know how that worked for young women.

"Well, there are plenty of trickster characters in lots of cultures. I wish I could be more help for you there, but I don't have the historical perspective." *Like Reine did,* I added mentally.

"No worries. That's what school is for. Like, look at these." She clicked on a section called, "Interdisciplinary Courses," and one of the first to pop up was a class called Appalachian Myths and Legends from Native American Perspectives through Modern Tales.

"That sounds like a big course."

"Yes, it spans two semesters. You have to apply to get in."

"Who's the professor?" I expected it would be some showoff who loved legends of cryptids and had thrown the Native American in there to satisfy some university requirement. Yes, I'd added a dash of cynical to my coffee that morning, but when she clicked on the *Instructor* link, a picture and bio popped up. A hirsute, dark-skinned man grimaced from a picture taken in the woods, and his name read, "Peter Grand-Pied, PhD, Professor of Humanities and Interdisciplinary Studies."

"Grand-Pied?" I asked. "That's taking it a bit too far, isn't it?"

Kestrel cocked her head at me. "What do you mean?"

"Grand-Pied is French for 'big foot.'"

She smirked. "I'm definitely going to sign up for this class. He sounds like he has a good sense of humor. Do you know him or know of him?"

"I don't know." The name tickled something buried deep in my brain. "If he's a paranormal like us, then we'll have a file on him at the CPDC. Speaking of which..." I checked my watch. "I need to go in."

"Why?" She gazed up at me. "I haven't finished picking my classes yet."

I ruffled her hair like I had since she was little, and she swatted my hand. "Text me when you figure it out. Remember, I didn't go to University in this country." Or this century, but she didn't need to know how old I was.

"You trained at Georgia."

"In the vet school. My undergrad was in England." At least if nothing else, we paranormals were good at faking transcripts for ourselves and each other. I'd have to ask my mother if we needed to get The Aerie residents hooked back into that system now that they were going to start having babies again.

"All right, I'll let you know if I need help with anything." She tucked her feet under her, and I saw she hadn't been wearing socks or slippers on the cool floor. Should I have noticed? I didn't have any experience with parenting, especially not a young adult. Shouldn't she have the sense to cover her feet?

I rubbed my face, and the stubble pricked my fingers. Basic self-care thoughts could be a challenge when one was grieving. This I knew all too well.

"Call me if you need me urgently. Otherwise, you know where everything is."

"Will do." She kept her gaze on her laptop but gave me a thumbs-up.

I turned and walked into the house, stopping to refill my coffee. I felt guilty for leaving her, but she didn't need me to hover. She could take care of herself with her newly found magic. What would she do with it when surrounded by humans?

That's what really worried me.

WHEN I WALKED into the CPDC an hour later, I found all traces of the chaos of the previous two months had been erased. They'd pieced the lab back together, and techs moved among the benches as though nothing had happened. The bullet holes in the walls had been repaired and painted over.

The biggest thing to be the same as previously, and which shouldn't have been, was Lucius Cimex, the man who had shot Kestrel's mother, allegedly while under the influence of an invisible creature, sitting at his desk in the director's office.

4

REINE

Scotland, 16 April, 1746

Rhys leaned on me, heavier with every step we took. Or perhaps our power weakened along with our connection to our home in Faerie. Unlike many of the soldiers, we didn't leave a trail of smeared blood behind us, but we might as well have as Fae magic drained from us with every second.

"Are we human now?" Rhys' question came out garbled through his mangled mouth. "I taste my blood. I didn't know Fae could taste their blood."

"We've always been able to taste our blood, Rhys. Maybe your tongue is healing." I hoped the rest of his mouth was, too.

"If it is, I want it to stop. It's hurting." He stumbled, and I caught him and held him until he regained steadiness. No matter what he'd done, he was still my little brother, and I'd protect him. I'd spent more time than he in the Earth Realm, so I knew how human society worked. I feared his injury would pose the least danger to him of all the challenges we'd have to face as exiles.

Exiles. We'd heard of them, of course—Fae who had

displeased my grandmother and who disappeared as a result. Would we find some? And if we did, would they help us? Anyone who knew the royal family of the light Fae would recognize us, so I had little hope. No one held a grudge like a Fae.

"All right, we can continue," he said. "Are we close?"

"I think so. I gave her a charm to keep the cottage hidden. Shhh, let me listen for it." Although my powers were muted, I could still find spells I'd set. They called to me with their own familiar music, like wind chimes of a specific frequency. Each person's blood had its own tone as well. I'd learned as a healer to listen to it to help me diagnose and heal those who were fortunate enough to have non-life-threatening illnesses. As for the others... I couldn't interfere if they were close to death or had something terminal like cancer that had spread too far. After a certain number of incidents that had made it into fairy tales, the supernatural community had rules about how much we Fae could meddle in the affairs of humans.

Yet another reason to lie low.

We staggered along for another mile and paused again for me to close my eyes and search. The chill breeze carried the scent of fresh-turned earth and the tinkling of my spell. The witch must have been doing her spring planting. I led Rhys in that direction. We met with a wall of invisible resistance, and I whispered the words to allow us through the barrier.

The air inside the bubble caressed my cheeks with its warmth, and the witch's cottage glowed silver in the moonlight. Cloud shadows played across its thatched roof and garden. Each bed had been carefully lined with river stone so the plants wouldn't creep into other beds and mix with unplanned results. Indeed, as my nose had told me, the bed Irina kept for plants that only grew for a season had been cleaned out and the earth turned.

We hobbled up the walk, and I knocked on the door. The high-pitched keening of a woman's wail floated out to me.

Rhys finally lifted his head, and the moonlight silvered the tips of his hair and the edges of his wound. "What in Hades is that?"

"A woman in labor." I knocked again. "Irina is the local midwife."

Indeed, the witch opened the door and frowned at us. Her gray-streaked dark hair had escaped in wisps from her bun, and she wiped her hands on a cloth. "Oh! Your Highness. To what do I owe the pleasure?" Her words held the courtesy due a high Fae, but her tone betrayed her weariness and wariness.

"We've run into trouble. I need you to help my brother and shelter us for the night."

Another noise came from inside—a long groan.

"I'm busy. You're welcome to come in and wait, but it may be a while." She stepped back, and her eyes widened when she saw the long slash along the side of Rhys' face. Her lips thinned, and she cut her eyes at me with a brief shake of her head. I got the message—Rhys' injury was beyond her skill. There went that hope, miniscule as it had been since we both knew I had the superior healing ability. Or at least I had before my exile.

"Tough labor?" I inclined my head toward the back bedroom. At least I wasn't the only one having a bad night.

Irina nodded, and the corners of her mouth pulled into a frown. "The baby is turned wrong, and I fear that the cord may be wrapped around its neck."

"Irina?" a woman's voice called. "Are you coming back? The pain, it's—" Her sentence devolved into another groan that expressed more than words could.

Irina glanced over her shoulder then back at me. "If I'm going to shelter you, I need your help. Your *unrestricted* help." She knew my rules, our rules, of non-interference. And I couldn't risk angering any more Fae, not in my newly tenuous position.

"No. If the others knew I'd broken the agreement..."

"You'd have had no problem taking advantage of a human in a vulnerable situation if she had something you wanted. Why are you surprised I'm doing the same?"

Rhys snorted. "She has a fair point, Sis. Give her what she wants. What choice do we have?"

I'd seen the shadows prowling outside. "Very well," I huffed. I almost told her I wasn't as strong as I had been even a few hours previously, but I had no desire to reveal my vulnerability. Who knew what she would ask or do next?

I followed her into the back bedroom, and the slick iron scents of blood, amniotic fluid, and fear assailed my nose. The mother lay on her side, and her swollen belly rippled with contractions. She looked up at us, her eyes wide with panic and the certainty she and her child were meeting their doom. I'd seen the same look in the eyes of animals cornered by predators. Her dark blonde hair lay slick against her pale skin.

"Who is she?"

"The wife of one of the soldiers. I didn't ask which side. She didn't volunteer."

After the massacre, I didn't blame the woman for keeping her identity close. She studied me and finally spoke in gasps. "What is... A Bain Sidhe... Doing here? They don't come... Inside."

The wife of an Irish soldier, come to help their Scottish allies, then. Why had she traveled so far in her state? Or had they lived here already?

I walked to her and clasped her hand. Her pulse beat fast against my fingers, and my healer training and instincts made me say, "We need to get the baby out of you. Both your hearts are failing. Do you understand me?"

She swallowed, then nodded.

"What are you thinking?" Irina's tone said she knew the answer but didn't like it.

"They don't have much time." Indeed, their double aura flickered like a sputtering candle. "Bring me your sharpest knife."

Irina nodded. I ignored the clenching feeling in my gut of disobedience to one of the principles that had been drilled into me—*don't save the truly dying*. And as talented as Irina was, these two would cross the veil if left to her.

"What do you ask in payment, Fae?" The woman's voice had grown clearer, and I snatched the knife from Irina.

"She's approaching the Last Crossing. Do you have any whiskey?"

"Yes, hold on."

There wasn't time. I leaned over to the woman and locked my gaze to hers. "Irina is paying your price for sheltering me. I'm going to say a sleep spell, and when you wake, you'll be holding your bairn."

She nodded, and I placed my hand on the crown of her head. Her eyes closed, and her and the baby's auras dimmed to an almost imperceptible glow.

"I'm not letting go yet," I muttered and moved with Fae speed to perform the Cesarean procedure. The lack of blood from the incision told me that the mother had been bleeding heavily for a long time. By the time Irina had returned with the whiskey, I held the surprisingly quiet infant, who looked up at me with big gray eyes. Her hair lay damp against her skull, but I could see the beginnings of red curls. My entire body tingled as I smiled down at this little one, whose aura now shone with the optimistic brightness of a new life snatched from the shadows.

"And the mother?"

I'd stitched her up as best I could, and she lay sleeping fitfully. "If she makes it through the night, may live, but probably not." I looked down again at the infant, then handed her to Irina to clean her up. "Take care of this one. She's special."

"I will."

Rhys and I left the next morning before we could find out whether the mother lived. I had given her as much as I could with my waning strength, which amounted to little more than a Fae blessing. But sometimes a blessing was enough.

As for the child...surely preserving an innocent life negated the rules against interference.

5

______

DOSSIER: PRINCESS REINE OF THE LIGHT FAE

S cotland, 17 April, 1746

Report by Sir Gerald Brigadine, First Regiment of the Silver Arrow, Tracker Division

Dear Sir, I hope this letter finds you well. I am writing the day after the glorious victory over the savages at Culloden, where the slaughter of the Highlanders, traitors, and werewolves—and those who were all three—will be sung of for centuries.

As you are aware through your orders, I did not take part in the battle itself. In fact, I followed your directions and sought after the witch who had defied your attention the prior year. She had married one of the savages and was great with child. She left an easy path to follow, although she had taken great pains to conceal her meanderings through the woods and scrub. I waited outside another witch's hovel, which had been hidden by a spell. The only way I could see it was through the blessing of the medal you had given me. At a little after midnight, a man and a woman arrived at the cottage and passed through the spell without difficulty. I waited to see what would happen, and the witch Irina admitted them without argument.

I crept to the window that I presumed belonged to the back bedroom, from which I heard the crying and groaning of a woman in labor. Before I could go through and snatch the target, the witch brought the new stranger to her, and I overheard a most odd conversation. The target addressed her as Fae, and from the racing of pinpricks along my skin, I felt her magic. She's a powerful one, my lord. I don't know what your target did to attract the attention of the high Fae, but apparently, she did, for the Fae saved the child and blessed the mother. The strangest thing—after the babe had been pulled from the mother's body, from what I could gather, as I could not see inside, the infant made no sound, as though it knew I waited outside and urged the discretion of its elders.

I waited in the newly dug garden until morning, when the Fae and her companion left. While I am sure you would have no trouble facing down such a creature, I lack the requisite ability and knowledge for dealing with them. I crept back to my station behind some trees, yet still inside the protective spell. Then a wondrous thing happened. The spell disintegrated, leaving the ruins of the witch's house. The gardens went from perfectly trimmed to overgrown and dying, and the house drooped and aged in a matter of seconds. I raced inside looking for the target so I could fetch her and the babe for you.

I found naught but a skeleton lying in the back bedroom, and the witch and the babe nowhere to be seen in spite of much searching among the now-brittle sticks of furniture, cobwebs, and dust.

I pray your forgiveness for failing in my mission. I can assure you, at least, that the wife of your enemy is dead. As for the child, which may or may not be yours via the law of First Night Privilege, I am afraid I have no leads. Please forgive me, your most humble servant,

. . .

Sir Gerald Brigadine
  First-Order Wizard
  Order of the Silver Arrow

6

———

REINE

e dashed into the witch's cottage, which lay in a decrepit state as though no one had entered in centuries. Most of the small objects that had been inside had decayed into dust and powder, and the spiders made merry with their decorating. Lonna sneezed, and Selene frowned.

Lonna checked her watch. She wore an analog piece, not one of those little computer things. "They should have sent help by now. Let me see if they tried to call."

We all pulled out our phones and cursed in our respective ways when we saw we had no signal.

"What is this place?" Selene trailed a finger through the dust on what had been the witch's worktable in the main room.

"It was a witch's cottage," I replied. "I..." I shook my head. "It's too complicated to explain." While the condition of the cottage didn't surprise me due to its age, something about its pattern seemed strange. What had become of Irina? She'd disappeared after that fateful night, and the other witches in her coven had thought she'd fled with the baby, since it turned out she belonged to a high-ranking officer in the Highlander army. Or had she? There had been a barbaric custom of the lord of the land claiming newlywed women on their wedding night, raping them, and then sending them back to their husbands, subdued and often pregnant. I shuddered at the thought. Although I had seen many babies and treated my share of children as part of my medical training, none stood out in my memory like that one did.

"You knew the witch." Lonna cocked her head at me, then grimaced. "What happened?"

I sketched out the story, leaving out any details that indicated I had broken the rules and saved a baby that would have died otherwise, although I didn't know that with certainty. That's what I told myself, anyway.

Lonna continued to rub her neck as she listened.

In case she'd forgotten, I told her, "I can help you. I'm a physician, and I have healing powers."

"No thank you," she said, too quickly.

Selene turned from where she'd been watching at the window. "It's all right. She's telling the truth, and I don't know that I would have been able to run if she hadn't helped me with my knee."

Lonna shook her head and added an extra dollop of firmness to her "no, thank you." Fear flashed through her light green eyes.

"You can't be afraid of me." Although a Fae queen should relish the thought that humans feared her, I wanted to help them. Perhaps Lonna had transferred her fear about her missing husband—and my friend—Max to fear about what I'd do to her. That thought sparked another question. "You can't think there's history between me and Max."

Her lips twisted into a rueful smile. "I know there's history, but mostly in the sense of time. I'm aware that you're much older than he and Gabriel, and they've lived longer than human lifespans." The sun had dipped below the tops of the trees, although sunset was still a ways off as we traversed the bright path of the year between Beltane and the solstice. She rubbed her upper arms with the chill the new shadows brought to the cabin. Cobweb curtains thickened the gloom.

Selene wandered around and poked at the furniture. "You said you were here the night after the Culloden battle?"

"Yes." I shivered remembering the terror of my banishment from Faerie and the sense of my powers draining with each hour, both due to the exile and because it was harder to 'recharge' without going back home. At least now, as queen, I held on to them longer, although the reason had been lost to history. Perhaps the Fae queen had previously gone to other realms on diplomatic missions in the distant past and needed to keep her powers, so whatever governed the balance of magic had allowed it.

"So that was, what, two hundred years ago?" She pinched the edge of the table, which left her fingertips dusty but didn't crumble.

"Two-fifty plus," Lonna said. "It was mid-1700s. Pre-United States."

I shook my head. Americans did like to reference others' history to their own.

Selene frowned and rubbed her fingers together. "No matter how well-made the furniture was, it should be crumbling. Think about it—it's been here in this windowless house where it would be exposed to the elements."

"But there's dust," Lonna pointed out.

"Yes, but being in a magical space would explain why our phones don't work even though we're close to Inverness and the highway."

I opened my senses to try to figure out what had happened, but I couldn't focus between my travel fatigue and the sense of not-rightness. Underneath, the suspicion I'd somehow been responsible ran like an invisible river of guilt. But I didn't do guilt.

"What do you think, Reine?" Selene asked.

"I...don't know." I hated saying the words. "I agree something's off here."

Lonna checked her watch again. "More importantly, do you think you can get us out of here so we can call for help? Or can you do it magically? You're the most powerful of all of us."

"I'm not sure how much I can manage after keeping us from being killed in the crash, healing myself and Selene, and then hiding our trail as we ran." I really hated admitting to my weakness, especially since the ancient witch Grylja had tried to take advantage of some mental cracks I had since shored up—I hoped. There I'd had Lawrence, Rhys, and other friends to support me. Here I had two women who were rightly suspicious of me and who couldn't lend me the power I needed.

"Will you be better after resting?" Selene asked. "How long do you need?"

"A few hours. I'll see what I can find to help." Then it occurred to me, "Lonna, did anyone know where you were? Will they come looking? You were speaking to them when we ran, right?"

She nodded and crossed her arms. "The car should have sent a signal to the ILR when it crashed, but I don't know how much good that will do us. And I was speaking to the Lycan Village dispatcher, not the ILR."

Selene clapped her hands together. "That means they could be out there looking for us right now. Or Gavin could!"

Lonna and I exchanged glances. Perhaps neither of us wanted to say anything since Selene had appeared to have suffered the worst shock.

Lonna murmured, "I'm betting they shot Gavin."

Selene bit her lip. "Did you see them do it?"

"No, but he would have followed us if he'd survived."

I turned to Lonna. "Who knew where you two would be and why?"

"Only a few people, but I get what you're saying."

"Yes. You have a traitor at the ILR."

IN SPITE of the prickly mattress and the absence of a purring grimalkin on my chest, I drifted off quickly. It briefly occurred to me that the straw that poked me should have rotted long ago. It was yet another strange thing about the day, but I couldn't waste the energy analyzing it. If I wanted to get us out of here, I needed to conserve my strength and recharge.

I sensed the wind-chime sparkle of the magic. How could I not? I'd given it to the spot centuries before. The question was, what had happened to Irina and the woman who had sought help with her birth? And what of the babe? Had mother and child lived or died? Not knowing the end of that story made me feel like I was missing a big piece of the puzzle that was my current existence.

When I opened my eyes into a dream, I found myself in a place I hadn't expected—Agnes' office in The Aerie. Like Lawrence's mother, the space itself offered a no-nonsense atmosphere aside from the small bar to the side. I sat on the couch, and when I looked over to the bar again, Agnes stood there mixing a couple of drinks.

"Old-fashioned?" She handed one to me without waiting for my response.

I took a careful sip. Often in dreams, food and drink didn't have much, if any taste, but the savory-sweet flavor of the cocktail warmed my tongue and esophagus. I changed the alcohol to water when it hit my stomach. The last thing I needed was to be intoxicated.

Agnes took a seat across from me. "How is it?"

"Good. *Slainte*."

"Cheers." We clinked glasses.

We both sipped, and she gave me one of her mom looks, as Lawrence called them. Considering my own mother had tried to kill me more than once, I straightened my spine and prepared to flee. Although Agnes had helped me out of a tight spot, and she and I had come to a truce of sorts, I still didn't trust her.

"Where are we, really?" I asked, both for information and out of hope that Lawrence would find me in this liminal space. Would he appear like his mother had when my gaze returned to different spots? No such luck.

"He's not here," she said. "And we're in the Collective Unconscious, as far as I can tell. I brought you here myself, although I'm not sure how. The witch's power still lingers in pockets, and sometimes we can find it and use it briefly."

I narrowed my eyes and focused on her. She wore a navy-blue pantsuit, and the right pocket glowed white.

"You've found some witch stones, you mean."

She answered with her usual directness. "Yes. In the cave."

"That's fine. They're not that powerful in the waking world. Don't let kids get hold of them, though. There's no telling what they'll try to conjure in their dreams." I'd heard about my grandmother's attempt to negotiate with nightmare creatures, and I didn't want careless gargoyles to give them an alternate conduit to the mundane reality.

"There aren't any kids to do so aside from the one young man, but thank you for the warning."

"What did you call me here for? More than to talk about what Grylja left you. If you don't mind, I'm trying to rebuild my strength."

She leaned forward, her shoulders slumped, and the effort of maintaining the connection flickered as a grimace over her face. "I have a warning for you."

"Does it have something to do with a bunch of bad guys in a car trying to chase me down and kill me? Because I've already found them."

She sipped her drink before answering. "It could be. Your enemies are more numerous than you know, and there is a powerful force behind them."

"Who is it?" I had my suspicions.

"I can't say, only that it's someone who doesn't share my values." She fixed me with a direct stare. "The values you came up against when you were here."

In that case, she must mean my mother or one of her allies. I'd bumped up against Agnes' desire to protect The Aerie, but more than that, to keep her own children safe. Fae didn't care as much about their children once they grew to be relative adults who asserted their own opinions.

And Agnes would only warn me if she thought Lawrence might also be in danger.

"I see." Now I leaned forward. "What does she have over you, Agnes? Why are you scared of her?"

"Who says I'm scared?" But when I looked beyond her Collective Unconscious illusion using my Fae sight, the fear showed on her face in the tightness of her jaw and the high color of her cheeks.

"I do. I can see your true self here. Don't forget that I'm a queen as well, and therefore I'm asking you, queen to queen, ally to ally, what does my mother have over you? Perhaps I can protect you."

"How could you possibly protect me? You're stuck in your own prison, although you refuse to see it. I love my son, but I don't love that you're using him as an excuse to not take your throne, not fully."

"Loose ends," I replied with a sigh. "There are still too many loose ends."

"Yes, and you're so focused on the loose threads at the edges of the tapestry that you're missing the unraveling in the middle. Take care, Queen Reine of the Light Fae. Your land needs you more than my son."

I didn't have to peer through her illusion to see how much the admission pained her, and my already high respect for her increased. If she was willing for me to break her son's heart, she must truly see a threat. Or perhaps the wisdom earned from her own heartbreak meant she would prefer that Lawrence know I was alive and unreachable instead of mourning my death.

"Thank you, but I need to know—what has she threatened you with?"

"You shouldn't have to ask. Her influence reaches far in this world, and we are at a fragile point right now with the lifting of Grylja's curse and the ability of our kind to reproduce again. The Aerie needs to be left alone."

"And she's going to point unwanted attention toward you if you don't play by her rules." Now those were terms I could understand. And they were also something I couldn't do much about. Information once released spun out of control.

She didn't respond in the affirmative, but she lifted her drink in a toast to my astuteness. "Go. Figure all this out. I'll support you as much as I can."

I bowed my head, something a queen never did to another. "Thank you. I am in your debt for the warning."

Hades. Just when I had enough to deal with, I was going to have to manage my mother, too.

"Oh, I can give you one word, Reine. Do you know what a Cimex is?"

7

LAWRENCE

I considered trying to cover my surprise, but Lucius Cimex's gaze locked on mine. He inclined his head to someone else in the room, and two burly, dark-suited shifters—neither of whom were Corey—walked into the hall and flanked me.

"Lucius, I didn't expect to see you."

"Nor I you, Lawrence. Aren't you supposed to be watching over young Kestrel Graves? How is she?"

Although he hadn't been in the role of CPDC director for months, he could still make me feel like I'd been caught out at something, that I'd broken some rule. I reminded myself that I didn't need to answer to him as my boss. In fact, I didn't even need this job, which I'd only kept for leads about who had killed my father and because it allowed me to bury my feelings in work I found meaningful. So why the escort?

"She's as well as can be expected. About to start at UGA since she's not going back to the PBI. What brings you back?"

He waved his hand above his head. "The powers that be pardoned me since I wasn't acting of my own agency when I shot Dr. Graves."

Dr. Graves, not Beverly. Not the woman he'd been obsessed with. Had he truly been acting according to the will of the soul-eater, or had he used it as an excuse to shoot her out of jealousy and the desire to keep their secrets? I merely nodded, though.

"Well, welcome back. If you'll excuse me, I have work to do." I turned toward the back wing and the registry of supernatural creatures when the two guards blocked me.

Cimex chuckled, not a pleasant sound. "Not so fast, Lawrence. I have a question for you."

I turned back. "Yes?"

"I'm aware that you haven't been around the office due to taking care of Kestrel. Such a tragedy, her father being killed in that 'automobile accident.'"

I swallowed and tried not to react. "I had some things to take care of."

"Yes, and did those things include the attractive Fae Reine? I heard she's queen now."

"Yes."

"Your partnership must have gone over well with her family. Speaking of which, I'm also aware that gargoyles don't have much in the way of family—that the mythical conclave called The Aerie doesn't actually exist, at least not in our records."

Up to a few weeks prior, I would have been able to deny knowledge of The Aerie, but his words loosened an avalanche of dread that tumbled through my torso.

"I concur that it's not in our records."

"But is it true that it doesn't exist? I've never known you to be a liar, Lawrence, and I can see the question makes you uncomfortable."

So much for that stone face Reine teased me about. "I am not at liberty to say anything about The Aerie, whether it exists or not."

"I see. Well, as nice as it is to have you back, I'm going to put you on administrative leave so you can work on sorting out the

Graves' affairs and support Kestrel as she adjusts to life without her parents."

"Very well, sir. I'll just stay the day and then not return tomorrow."

"Oh, no, that's not how this works. If you'd like to have a conversation with me about The Aerie, I'll be happy to allow you to stay. Otherwise, you're dismissed effective immediately."

The two shifters grabbed my arms. I scowled at them and asked, "What happened to Corey?"

"Corey has been moved to a new post due to his involvement with Kestrel and demonstration of poor judgment."

Damn. Corey would have given me the fifteen minutes I needed in the Registry, but these two wouldn't. I bowed my head. "Very well. I'll be on my way, then."

"Yes, you do that."

They bundled me out, but when we passed through the lab, I caught the eye of Latonya, who'd also been influenced by the soul-eater and had worked with both John and Beverly Graves on their research. She met me in the parking lot a few minutes after I'd walked out.

"Lawrence! What happened? Have you been fired?"

"No, simply given a mandatory leave of absence, but I need you to do some research for me without Cimex knowing."

She firmed her lips and nodded before saying, "Anything. I can't believe they let him back after what happened to Beverly."

"I feel the same. I suspect there's something bigger than us going on." Like an angry Fae crown princess, but she didn't need to know that terrifying detail. "Can you look into a Professor Grand-Pied at UGA? I have some suspicions about him as well as what's been going on here."

"I'll do my best, but I don't know how well I'll be able to access the Registry. We're on strict need-to-know protocols as a security measure."

I should have figured. "All right. Don't risk yourself. Just please know that this is important."

She gave me a mock salute. "Aye aye, Doctor. I'll call you from home as soon as I find out anything."

"Thank you."

As she walked back in, I hoped I wasn't endangering her, but she had a good head on her shoulders, which was why I'd singled her out.

Next stop—home.

8

———

REINE

When I woke, I had no idea where I was. I blinked to make my surroundings come into focus and turned my head to find the leering rictus of a skeleton beside me on the bed.

My heart rate hit a thousand, and I screamed. The skeleton disappeared, but the mattress still showed an indentation like someone had been lying there. A wave of dizziness overtook me, and I clutched my head to stop the spinning and the wave of worry over why Sir Raleigh still hadn't appeared.

Lonna and Selene ran into the room.

"What is it?" Lonna asked. "I didn't know Fae could scream."

I scowled at her, as much of a scowl as I could manage around my heartbeat, which still galloped between my ears. I gulped a couple of deep breaths, but the disorientation didn't leave.

"Yes, we do, but it's rare. And I thought I saw a skeleton. And something else is wrong. Sir Raleigh should have come back to me by now."

Selene pressed her own hand to her chest. "You feel it too?"

"Yes." The trembling subsided enough for me to walk to the window and find the moon. Whereas it had been waning when I'd left Atlanta, now it shone full and so brightly the yard appeared illuminated by a silvery sun. I recalled the tarot card Veronica had painted to look like me, The Moon, and while this particular light felt familiar, I gleaned no warmth from it.

Could we be in the past? That would explain the skeleton and the indentation on the bed. But how had we gotten there?

"Is it safe out there?" Lonna, ever the practical one, asked.

"I don't know." I didn't know if it was safe in here, either, but I wasn't going to say that.

We walked into the main room, and Selene and Lonna gasped.

"It wasn't like this before." Selene grabbed her purse off the chair and backed as far away as she could without going back into the bedroom. The dusty, musty room of a few hours ago had been replaced by a cozy living space with drying herbs hanging from the rafters, a merry fire in the fireplace under a pot of simmering stew, and candles in the holders giving the room a cheery albeit dim glow.

My head spun through possible explanations. My heart, on the other hand, flip-flopped between the warmth of nostalgia and the cold dread we wouldn't be leaving this space easily, perhaps not even alive.

A pair of figures, one tall and one short, materialized in front of the fire. Irina looked like she always had with gray-streaked black hair, flint for eyes, and a no-nonsense stiffness to her mouth. She held the hand of a little girl of about five, who had the light copper hair of the Irish. She clutched a ragged dolly, whose blank bead eyes glittered.

Irina looked me up and down. It took me a minute to decipher her words through her thick, old-fashioned accent. "It's about time you showed back up here, Lady Reine. This one and I, we've been trapped for centuries."

Selene's hand went to her stomach, and Lonna and I exchanged worried glances.

Irina continued, "I'd hoped you would appear at some point and let us out of this existence. Now here you are in men's breeches and blouses."

"We had to eat the same thing every day," the girl added in her high-pitched little voice, and added with Irina's inflection, "For centuries."

"That sounds hard," Selene agreed. She reached into her purse and brought out a candy bar. "Would this help?"

The little girl looked up at Irina, who nodded. She let go of her guardian's hand and crept forward, stopping just out of reach and stretching forward on her tiptoes to snatch the snack and return to Irina. They both looked at it, and then the child tried to take a bite of it. The wrapper crinkled but didn't break.

"It tastes of nothing!" she wailed.

"Here, let me help you," Selene said and moved toward them, but Irina held the child to her.

"Don't come closer." She tossed the bar back at Selene. "I don't know what witchcraft you've used to trap us here, and now you try to give us food that isn't food. After I helped you, Princess."

"I didn't know, I swear."

"What is your name, little one?" Lonna asked.

Irina answered. "She knows better than to say in front of a Fae, Lady. 'Tis bad enough she knows mine."

"Please tell me what happened," I told her. I gestured to the table, around which the chairs had grown simple cushions. "May we sit?"

Irina nodded and pulled four fired clay bowls from one of the shelves. The clever potter had glazed them so the shadows of wisps of heather decorated the sides. "Are ye ready for some stew, child?"

The girl sighed. "Yes, Mum. Has the bread returned?" She

turned her wide green-blue gaze to Selene, whom she resembled. "Sometimes it appears, sometimes not."

"Bread can be tricky like that," Selene agreed, sitting, and the child grinned. I hid a laugh, although it seemed odd that Irina had claimed the child as her own. The mother had definitely died, then. But the skeleton had appeared to me, so what did that mean? Was her spirit caught in the time loop as well?

Lonna refused to take a seat. "We have bigger priorities, Reine. Remember?"

Irina and her ward both gasped.

"You dare address the princess so casually?"

Lonna sighed, and I sensed her patience waning. "Yes, because where we come from, we're mostly equals."

A scoff puffed from my chest. "That's news to me. I'm the queen of Faerie now, remember?"

"Some queen you are. We're trapped, remember?"

Selene leaned back so she could look out of one of the windows. "Was the moon supposed to be full tonight? I could have sworn not."

That introduced another level of complication—would Selene and Lonna have to change? What would Irina and her ward think?

Like Lonna said, bigger problems. Many of them.

I tried to ask in a circumspect way. "Do either of you feel it?"

"No." Lonna replied with a shake of her head. "Not like I should."

"Maybe a little," was Selene's response. "But it's not bad."

One of the smaller bubbles of tension in my chest popped. "Then we should focus on getting out of here."

"Good luck with that, Milady." Irina placed a bowl of stew on the table in front of the little girl. "We've been trying for..." Her brows creased. "A long time."

What could be keeping her and the child here in this suspended state? Did time pass so slowly here that only five years had gone by, while hundreds had passed in the outside world?

The familiarity of the scenario lanced through my gut with white-hot fear. This felt like what happened to humans in parts of Faerie, where time crawled, like in the Rip Van Winkle legend. And that meant I'd had something to do with it.

"When did it start, you being stuck?"

Irina inclined her head to the kid. "Since the night she was born."

So they hadn't disappeared. They'd been caught in a time bubble. And now so were we.

9

LAWRENCE

I tried to call Reine when I got home. She'd want to know what had happened and that something was up, but her phone went straight to voicemail. I knew that plane trips knocked her out after, so I didn't think anything of it, figuring she'd turned off her phone so she could sleep undisturbed. The connection between us, the one that felt like it was anchored behind my breastbone, remained steady, although I found myself plagued by a restlessness that went beyond the fact that I'd thought I was going to be working today and wasn't.

Screw her nap. I tried to call again with the same result.

Kestrel returned to the house with shopping bags in tow.

"What's all this?" My question might have come out more irritably than I anticipated because her expression hardened from curious to neutral. "I mean, looks like you did some shopping."

"Yeah, like we talked about. Stuff for my new apartment?"

"Right, sorry, I forgot."

"Since this morning? Is everything okay?"

"I don't know."

She didn't ask what I meant. "Hey, since you're home,

maybe we can drive up to Athens this afternoon, get the lay of the land."

Her idea sounded good, a necessary distraction, and it wasn't like I'd be away from my phone. "Sure, that sounds good."

A few hours later, we walked through the University of Georgia's main campus, headed for the building that housed sociology and a few other soft sciences. It sat across the street from the psychology building, which I'd learned from a previous investigation took up all six floors with various flavors of psychology and a clinic on the first floor. Would all that mental health research and the clinic be enough to help Kestrel through her dual grief?

She mostly managed to hide it, but her facial tension shifted with her mood, and I wanted to ask if she was wishing that she could ask one of her parents something or tell her mom about what she was doing. I agreed it was unfair she'd lost both. I'd known the pain of my father's death when I was young, and I couldn't imagine trying to manage without my mother.

"This is it," Kestrel said and pushed her sunglasses up to perch on her head. "Do you think he'll be in?"

"He's a university professor. Where else would he be?" Except wandering the wood of North Georgia, or maybe that was a cousin. I'd heard Blairsville was a hotspot for bigfoot activity.

A young woman about Kestrel's age approached us before we could go in. She wore her blonde hair back in a ponytail that swished as she walked, and she carried a textbook and notebook. "Who are y'all looking for? It's pretty dead in there."

Kestrel's shoulders lifted and dropped, and she smiled, although the corners of her mouth remained tight. "Professor Grand-Pied."

I moved back a step to let Kestrel take the lead.

"Oh, yeah." The student checked her phone. "He should be finishing up a class in the journalism building."

"But he's a sociology professor?"

The young woman grinned. "That building has bigger classrooms, and since it's a summer seminar, it's joint sociology with psychology." She dropped her voice. "Just a warning—he's not exactly the friendliest, but he knows his stuff."

"Thanks. Which way is the journalism building?"

"It's the big one next to psychology."

"Okay, thank you for your help."

We moved that way, and although campus stood relatively quiet due to the summer season, the energy shifted when classes in the nearby buildings let out. I could almost see Kestrel struggling not to hunch her shoulders and instead to feign confidence. It reminded me how young she was.

When we rounded the corner to the courtyard between psychology and journalism, the professor drew my eye immediately. He stood a head over the tallest students, and he wore his hair shaggy with a bushy beard that looked well-cared for but probably hadn't had a trim in months. If I'd been suspicious that one of the elusive dimension-walkers had somehow managed to embed himself in a university setting, where quirky and eccentric would be expected, now I had certainty. And I wouldn't need Cimex or anyone to give me permission to talk to him since I was on a personal mission.

If I'd identified him as a Bigfoot, he'd certainly recognize me as a gargoyle, so I held back and ducked into the shadows.

I urged Kestrel, "Go and talk to him. You're in public, so you should be safe."

Her brows almost kissed in confusion. "What should I say? And why can't you come with me?"

I answered her questions in reverse order. "He'll feel threatened if I approach him directly. I can tell what he is, and I'm guessing he hasn't encountered any gargoyles in a long, long time, if ever, so I don't want to spook him. This is an initial meeting, so introduce yourself and tell him you're transferring over in the fall, and you're interested in his class."

The professor edged away from the students who'd engaged him.

"Go on. Use your PBI experience for gentle interrogation."

I hated to bring up the Paranormal Bureau of Investigation, but Kestrel might as well use her strengths. While the Fae were known for obfuscation, ours had ripped the lid off many a secret, but the tragic results didn't mean Kestrel had to forget all she'd learned and start over.

"Okay."

She walked over to him, and I took several deep breaths to keep myself from following her and assuming a protective stance. My calves clenched so hard they ached, and I had to remind myself not to lock my knees. My inner gargoyle stirred. I sternly told myself nothing would happen—I was approaching the professor as a potential ally, not an enemy.

Uncertainty swirled through me, though. At the CPDC, I'd had the opportunity to encounter and work with most para-normal types. The Bigfoot kind presented a big unknown, and nothing bothered me like lack of data.

Like where the hell was Reine? She still hadn't returned my calls.

Kestrel approached him, and he started to move past her, but stopped. She had her back to me, so I couldn't tell what she said, but his nostrils flared. I'd almost forgotten how *she* would appear to a fellow paranormal now that she'd come into her powers. If gargoyle encounters were rare, trickster ones were practically unheard of.

The courtyard cleared—must have been time for the next class. Kestrel and Grand-Pied moved toward me, and I tensed my upper back so my wings wouldn't sprout and herald a change. *No threat, no threat, no threat.*

Kestrel's forced smile had returned, and Grand-Pied scowled.

"As I was saying, I'm really looking forward to taking some of your classes in the fall. I've already had Intro to Sociology, so what do you think I should take next?"

He stopped at the edge of the shadow and growled, "I think you should take your pet gargoyle and go home, Trickster."

That did it. I managed to keep my gargoyle in check, but the protective godfather came to the surface.

I stepped into the light. "Well met, Dimension Walker."

"What is this? Are you trying to trap me? I haven't hurt anyone or caused any mischief. I take no responsibility for the teases in Blairsville." He rubbed his eyes. "Distant relatives."

I held up my hands. "No, no. I'm here with my goddaughter, whom you've just met."

His bushy brows danced closer. "You're a gargoyle with a trickster goddaughter? How did that happen?"

Seeing an opening, I suggested, "How about we take you to lunch, and we can explain?"

He looked at his watch again. "Can't. I need to meet with a graduate student." Then he looked up. "No time. See you in the fall. Take the 201 class."

"Wait, I need your help with something else."

"So does everybody. No time."

He stalked off, leaving me and Kestrel shivering in the late spring sunlight.

She rubbed her arms. "What is this feeling?"

"That's what it's like to be near a dimension-walker, a being who's not entirely of this world. The humans don't necessarily feel it, but you could see they're not comfortable around him."

Then she said something that shouldn't have surprised me. "It must be lonely for him. I wonder who his graduate student is and how they can stand it."

"Indeed. I sense we've only scratched the surface of

Professor Grand-Pied's secrets. What does your training suggest we do next?"

She rewarded me with one of the only smiles I'd seen from her recently. "Follow him, ambush him into another conversation. Wear him down."

"We can try." But I didn't know how well we'd be able to do that with a being that powerful.

10

REINE

Although I'd had a nap, it hadn't been real rest due to my being summoned to a dream conversation with Agnes. I should've suspected something had gone awry with the ease she'd been able to do so. Now I had a big puzzle, and my jet-lagged and travel-scrambled brain crashed when I attempted to come up with a solution. I should've focused on an explanation.

"Reine...?" I imagined Lonna using that tone on her daughter when she'd done something naughty she tried to hide from her mum.

"Yes, Lonna."

"Why are they stuck here? Can we help them?" Translation: *can we get out ourselves?*

"I don't know. As I told you, I set up a protection spell around this cottage so that only those with good intentions could find it. There was nothing in the spell that had anything to do with not being able to leave."

"What happens when you've tried?" Selene asked Irina.

"We've come back here, as though the path twisted under our feet and changed our direction."

"Mummy, bread! And butter. That's new." The little redhead ran to the small table beside the fireplace, on which a loaf of rustic bread now sat along with a plate with what looked like soft, freshly churned butter.

"That's lovely dear. Maybe these nice ladies coming to visit have made something change about the spell that traps us here." The look Irina gave me told me she'd lost a good deal of the respect she'd once had for me, although she'd still follow protocol out of fear of what I would do if offended. I wanted to tell her I wasn't that Fae anymore, but I doubted she'd believe me.

Irina pulled a knife from the drawer and brought the bread to the table. Instead of applying the sharp, serrated edge to the crust, she wheeled around and held it to Selene's throat.

I stilled, and Lonna gasped.

Now Irina's gaze held desperation when she turned it on me. "Go see for yourself what happens when you try to leave. And if you don't come back, I'm going to slit this lovely lass' throat."

Selene's complexion went paper white under her freckles. "Reine, what's going to happen to me if she kills me? Will I come back?"

"I don't know. Child, do you?"

She pressed her lips together.

"Very well, then."

Lonna appeared torn as to whether she wanted to come with me or stay and protect Selene.

Irina solved her quandary. "You stay here, too. I don't trust her. Or you. Sit there."

Lonna obeyed and plopped on the seat across from Selene.

"I'll do what I can, I promise," I said, but I wasn't sure to whom. This situation had gone sideways, but if I'd been eating the same thing for several years—with no dessert—I'd be stabby, too.

I walked into the cool air of the mid-spring evening, which still held the remnant of winter's bite. It lacked the softness of leftover summer warmth, as I would have expected for mid-May. But this wasn't mid-May. If this was after the Battle of Culloden, it would be late April. A disturbing realization hit me—after living in the Earth Realm for so long, would I become bored with the eternal spring of the land of the light Fae? And once I claimed my throne for good, would I be able to leave for personal reasons?

A movement at the edge of the garden made me turn in that direction, but even with my Fae vision, I had no luck. Perhaps my tired mind's desire for something to change the monotony had tricked me. My curiosity led me in that direction, and I found footprints in the soil that appeared to have been made by a man's shoes. Interesting. I attempted to walk into the woods beyond that spot, but as Irina said, I found myself facing the cottage again although I hadn't changed my direction. A stroll around the garden and many dizzying forced reorientations later, I had to agree with Irina's conclusions. Something had us trapped here, outside of the world we'd been in that afternoon. Although I'd saved Lonna and Selene's lives, I might have doomed them to eternal repetition, which could become anyone's hell.

I walked back inside and reported my findings.

Irina removed her knife from Selene's throat, and Selene slumped forward and put her head in her hands. Her shoulders shook with her sobbed release from mortal danger. Then she bolted to her feet and ran outside. I thought about chasing after her, but she couldn't go far.

I warned Irina, "I won't say I didn't understand your action, but if you do something like that again, I will smite you in front of your daughter."

The color drained from Irina's face, and the knife fell to the ground with a thud. "I understand, Princess."

"Reine, can I speak to you?" Lonna asked. "Alone."

I nodded. It was my turn to be scolded.

WITH THE COTTAGE only being two rooms, Lonna walked to the bedroom. She glanced out of the window.

"She's pacing in the garden. I should be out there comforting her, but I needed to talk to you first. What the hell, Reine?"

My brain slammed a shield in front of my heart, which also ached for Selene. I bit out the words, "Is this what you do at the ILR? Call people on to the carpet of your plush office when things don't go as planned?"

"What? No. This is an unusual situation."

I crossed my arms to double the shield. "I'm glad you appreciate that. Want to tell me why you're pissed at me? I saved your life, remember?"

"And then almost cost us Selene's. What's going on here? Who is Irina, really, and why are we stuck here?" She held up her phone. "There's no signal, which should be impossible because we've got ILR transmitters all over this area."

She must have squeezed one of the side buttons because her phone flashed a lock screen picture of Max holding their daughter, both of them with big smiles, before it went dark again.

Gods, I was an idiot. If my loved ones were in danger and stuck somewhere I couldn't help them, I'd be angry, too. But I still didn't appreciate her tone. I tried to bring the tension down with, "Look, if I knew, I'd tell you."

She didn't appear appeased. "You brought us here, so I thought you might have some clue."

"And you've been dealing with your lycanthropy and all the other weird stuff in our world for how long, Lonna? You, of all people, vargamore split between the worlds of werewolf and wizard, should know that sometimes the answers aren't right there for the plucking."

"You think I don't know that?" She threw her hands up in a classic Italian gesture of frustration. "But *you're* the expert here. *You're* the one with more knowledge than I'll ever have. All I want you to do is..." She trailed off with a frown.

"All you want me to do is, what? Magically zap us out of here? Make us invisible to the men who are hunting us in the woods outside? Somehow get a signal out to the ILR to come looking for us with a phalanx of wizards?"

All right, I could possibly do that last one since I'd managed to talk to Agnes, and I had seventy percent sureness that had been a real interaction and not a dream, judging from how I'd felt after. I didn't want to make any promises, though.

"I want you to do *something* so no one gets her throat slit or stuck in some dusty, decaying two-room cottage where we have to eat stew for eternity."

"I'm working on it."

"Well, work harder, and if you don't figure it out, then I'll have to. I'm giving you two hours."

"You're putting a deadline on me? Need I remind you that I outrank you in every way? I'm a ruler of a realm. I'm a physician. I'm a Fae, and you're a mere mortal."

"Regardless, sometimes you need to step aside and let someone else take the lead. Otherwise, you're a terrible queen."

That did it. I summoned my Fae magic, which I still had access to in an attenuated sense due to a protective muting mechanism. Doing magic in these liminal spaces risked tearing holes in the fabric of time, which would allow things to come through that would make our current nightmare appear as a pleasant summer afternoon daydream.

With a flick of my wrist, a glowing blue lasso appeared and settled over Lonna's head and around her neck. I didn't pull it, but she still clutched it, then said, "Fuck!" and shook her hands, which likely burned with the intensity of the cold.

"And sometimes you need to remember who you're talking to," I growled. "Now if you're going to help, give me something I can use."

She sighed, but her features didn't soften into acquiescence. If anything, her expression grew more defiant, and she spat, "Meg. The little girl's name is Meg."

I almost missed her answer because I caught a shimmering opalescent light in the corner of my vision. When I turned to look, it disappeared, but a familiar scent wafted through, of fresh flowers and the softness of a spring evening.

Homesickness twisted my heart, but I turned my attention back to Lonna. "Thank you." With another flick of my wrist, the lasso disappeared. She put her hands to her neck, which should have been frostbitten, but I'd kept the spell from hurting her.

Guilt surged through me in a sickening wave, and I straightened my spine so I wouldn't slump under its weight or curl around where it gnawed at my middle. Had I learned nothing in The Aerie? If it hadn't been for the cooperation of the others, I would've been toast. But still, I couldn't make myself tell her I was sorry for the power display, although I couldn't say why. The history between us, maybe? That she'd snared Max when I'd failed? That didn't make sense since I had Lawrence, I loved Lawrence, and the connection to him quivered with longing every time I thought of him, so I'd been trying not to.

Or did it come down to classic alpha female issues? I'd ask Selene, but I didn't want to bring her into the middle of this power struggle.

"I suppose that we've reached an agreement, then," I said in the softest tone possible.

"I suppose," she echoed in a skeptical tone.

I was about to try to convince her the way I should have

previously, but before I could say anything, a crash and three simultaneous screams made us run back into the main room.

We found Selene, Irina, and Meg behind the table, which had been upturned and the crockery broken in their haste to put something between them and the fireplace. Sparks flew from it but didn't set anything ablaze. If anything, they danced in dizzying corkscrew patterns with the flames, and the roaring had assumed the cadence of mocking laughter.

"Why didn't you run outside?" Lonna demanded, but she sounded like some of her fire had been dampened by our discussion.

"In case it will give us a clue to escape," Irina snapped back. "And these two wouldn't leave."

"I've seen something like it before," Selene argued. "Reine, it reminds me of when you did the scrying thing."

At her words, the flames and sparks swirled in a pattern eerily reminiscent of the shadow vortex that sometimes occurred before something appeared in a bowl of water or onyx mirror.

Meg turned her little face to me. Her eyes glowed slightly, and she told me in a tone too deep for her years, "It awaits your command, Your Highness."

I swallowed. Your Highness, not Princess. This was Fae magic.

"Show me the key to escaping this time bubble," I whispered, not sure what would happen.

The vortex swirled to cover the entirety of the fireplace's opening, and the flames then coalesced into a three-dimensional picture. Colors filled in, and a young woman with premature gray streaks at her temple placed something on a wooden table. We appeared to peer at her from within the hearth of a cottage similar to Irina's.

The memory struck me with an electric jolt through my brain. I had remarked on the similarity of her cottage to Irina's when Rhys and I had visited her.

"Do you recognize this?" Selene asked. I'd tried to remain still, but I should've figured that Selene's hyper empathy would pick up on my reaction.

"Yes, it's a scene from my past."

Lonna crossed her arms and asked, "How do we turn up the sound?"

"Hush," Irina said with a swatting motion of her hand. "Someone just knocked."

The woman walked out of the frame and returned with two hooded figures following her. I chewed my bottom lip because I recognized the defiant set of Rhys' shoulders and the desperate curl of my own, although I would never have admitted it. Indeed, when the two pushed back the hoods of their dark gray cloaks, they were revealed to be me and my brother back when we still hoped to return to Faerie soon. My hair still held some of its light blonde color, and I wore it back in a simple twist. Rhys' scar, the disfigurement that had kept us exiled from Faerie, practically glowed.

"I'm sorry, Milady, I cannot help you." The woman, Amarie, said in an apologetic tone. "One of my neighbors has accused me of sickening her pig and her child, and I cannot do anything to bring more suspicion of witchcraft on myself."

"Please, just look at his face and let me know if it's within your skill or not." The me in the picture smiled, and a rosy glow surrounded my form—my Fae glamour. "I would greatly appreciate it."

"Yes, Mistress," she responded dreamily. I closed my eyes as shame lanced through my middle. I wouldn't develop the ethics surrounding minor use of Fae power for another—well, I wouldn't think about that.

She placed her hand on Rhys' cheek and closed her eyes. He shot me an exasperated look, and I tilted my head at him. I could almost hear the secret conversation between us.

"This is a waste of time," he complained.

"Just allow her to do what she needs. This isn't only for you, remember?"

"Yes, as you remind me daily."

Perhaps I hadn't been the nicest to him at that time, either.

The witch dropped her hand. "I'm sorry, the damage is too deep. Although..."

"Yes?" We both leaned forward.

"There is a ceremony I could do at the full moon to illuminate the structure of the injury. As you've probably guessed if it's beyond your healing power, Lady, there's something different about it."

We both knew it wouldn't heal because it had been done with a blessed blade made of iron. But I'd grasped at any hope she would give us. Had I missed something?

The picture shifted to reveal the top of a hill. A few lights in the valley behind it showed us the town was asleep. Amarie built a small fire from green wood, and I channeled some power to it so the sticks would flame more quickly. She blew on them to ignite them higher, and then stood. She wore a dark, hooded cloak, and she whispered her spells. Every one of her movements betrayed the furtiveness of the scene and her own anxiety.

She stood motionless for several minutes, and with this wider perspective, I noticed the line of torches that came from the town and snaked up the hill behind us. I wanted to cry out, to warn the two Fae and the witch engaged in the diagnosis spell, but of course they wouldn't hear me.

"You there!" The yell jolted us out of our concentration. "What are you doing, witch?"

Amarie's voice shook, but she stood her ground. "I am no witch. Is it illegal for us to share tales around a fire on a bonny night like this?"

"She's a witch!" This was a female's voice. "She sickened my pig and my daughter, and now the illness is spreading to the neighbors."

"Swine flu or something similar," I whispered to my fellow observers. "Although I never found out where it came from."

"I am innocent," Amarie declared, then turned to me. "Help me."

Rhys and I exchanged glances.

"This is our fault," I said.

"She chose to help us."

"She's a healer. We can't resist a good puzzle."

"What do we do?"

"Fog spell. And run."

Darkness filled in the picture from the edges of the frame— the fog spell. When the gloom covered the entire rectangle, a glowing yellow Y shape lying on its side briefly appeared before the fireplace returned to its normal cheery appearance.

"What was that?" Lonna demanded simultaneous with Selene asking, "What happened to her?"

I chose to respond to Selene's question since I knew that answer. "Rhys and I, well, Rhys disappeared for a while after that attempt failed... I helped her to escape to Brittany, where she settled in another village. I don't know how her life turned after that."

Lonna tapped her lips. "That means that was an actual scene from your life, not some weird vision or dream?"

"Yes. It was part of my ongoing efforts to find healing for Rhys' face."

"What happened to it?" Meg asked, now back to her child-like self. I wanted to inquire about what had peered through her at me—could Troubadour have been trying to reach me?

"He got in a stupid situation and was ambushed, and someone cut him with a special blade."

"Meaning that he couldn't go back into Faerie," Lonna finished. "Not scarred like that."

"Correct." Although my grandmother had finally healed him, the situation still made anger curl at my solar plexus since my mother Maeve had kept me and Rhys from accessing our grandmother, which meant a centuries-long exile for us. That had given my mother plenty of time to attempt to convince my grandmother to take me out of line for the throne, since Maeve knew I would be a better queen. Or so I'd thought. What I'd done to Lonna—that had been a Maeve move. So had the glamour that nudged Amarie out of her ambivalence into attempting to help Rhys. What would have happened to her if we'd left her alone? No telling. Perhaps she would have been killed, perhaps she would have figured out a way to be left alone or move somewhere not so far from her original home.

Irina and I righted the table, and she gathered up broken crockery.

"I'm sorry," I told her and ignored Lonna's offended gasp. "I'll try to fix them for you."

"No need. All will be the same as it was when night falls again." She glanced toward the window, which showed the lightening sky of pre-dawn. "We only have an hour left here before we go to our non-slumber." Indeed, the longer she'd been there, the more tired she looked, and more gray streaks crept into her hair. Meg, however, looked the same. Another part of the mystery to figure out.

"How can we help you before you go?" Selene asked.

"Will you read Meg here a story?"

"Lonna, do you have anything on your phone?"

Lonna smiled, but sadness tightened the muscles around

her eyes. "Yes, I have a few kids' books downloaded on my e-reader app. Here."

Selene sat on one of the chairs, and Meg crawled on to her lap. She could have been Selene's child, their coloring was so similar, and I wished I could snap a picture so I could show Gabriel. Wait, I could. I took a surreptitious shot while Selene showed Meg the phone, and Meg's face lit with delight. Kids, no matter what era they lived in, loved shiny things.

"This is the story of *The Little Engine That Could*. Like you, he's in a tough situation."

"What's an engine?"

I hid a smile. That story would require more explanation than narrative.

"Okay, let's find something different. How about *Cinderella*?"

"All right. What's a Cinderella? Is that like a princess?"

"You'll see."

Lonna walked outside, and I followed her. At first, I didn't see her, but she emerged from the shadows at the edge of the woods. "You're right. I can't leave."

The waning light of the moon, which had dipped behind the trees, and the soft light on the cabin illuminated something shiny on her cheeks, which she wiped with the heels of her hands.

"I promise, I'm doing all I can."

She refused to meet my gaze. "I wish I could believe that. How do I know you're not acting in your Fae interests, and trapping us is part of some major plot?"

"Because..." I looked into the night and rubbed my chest. "I have someone I want to get home to as well."

A low chuckle startled both of us. I narrowed my eyes and activated my Fae sight. Indeed, someone stood at the edge of the clearing, but all I could make out was the stocky form of a man.

11

DOSSIER: PRINCESS REINE

S cotland, May 2, 1786

REPORT BY SIR GERALD BRIGADINE, First Regiment of the Silver Arrow, Tracker Division

DEAR SIR,

I hope this missive finds you enjoying your new position. Indeed, I hope it finds you at all. I continue to experience difficulty achieving my footing in the mundane timeline, and my life still skips. However, in my latest appearance, I found more evidence of the Princess Reine and Prince Rhys interfering with human lives.

I landed in the town square of a little village near the market cross. As before, no one seemed to notice me, and then they did. I must have appeared ill because one of the villagers directed me to the cottage of a witch, the village's healer. They warned me she had attracted some suspicion from a neighbor, who alleged the witch had caused the illness of a pig and a child. The witch apparently maintained her innocence, but I went forth to interrogate her anyway.

At her cottage, I found she already had two visitors, so I ducked around the side that backed up to an alley and let myself in through the bedroom window. Imagine my surprise when I saw the two Fae conversing with her about healing the prince's disfigurement. She appeared reluctant until Princess Reine employed her filthy powers, and, with a glamour, forced her will. I talked to the witch after they left—and after I had gone back out and in the normal way—and she acknowledged she'd felt the glamour but felt that doing a favour for a Fae would benefit her. I suspect the glamour was still active at that point.

I witnessed the hilltop Beltane ceremony and the village mob coming to capture and burn the witch. The two Fae created a thick mist, and all of them disappeared. I am writing this in hopes that I can send it before I, too, vanish, only to find myself at a different time and place.

Thank you for your patience with me, and if you could employ one of your wizards to rescue me from this spell, which I suspect is also the doing of Princess Reine or her brother, I would greatly appreciate it.

SINCERELY AND DESPERATELY,

Sir Gerald Brigadine

12

LAWRENCE

Kestrel and I grabbed an early dinner in Athens and verbally dissected the interaction with Professor Grand-Pied. Kestrel, being more emotionally intuitive, observed, "He wanted to be left alone. That's the sense I got from him."

"Tough gig to be a professor, then."

She thought for a few minutes. "No, he seemed fine with that part. He's just gruff. No, he didn't want to be treated as a supernatural being."

I thought back through the conversation and had to concur. "That means he's less likely to help with figuring out the Faerie atmosphere problem." Itchy frustration swelled in my chest and evoked the memory of the suffocating illness I'd developed after being in Faerie for a few days.

"There may be a way to get to him..." Her fingers did a thinking dance on the arm rest. "He mentioned a graduate student. Maybe I can get more information if I talk to them."

Again, I heard her PBI persona come through, but I didn't mention it. Despite her assertion of wanting to be a "normal person again," she fell back on it. It was hard to reject deeply ingrained training, but if I could do it and love the sister of the Fae who'd killed my father, then perhaps Kestrel could keep the useful parts of hers.

"Good idea. Do you know how to find them?"

She tapped on her phone. "Yes. Here she is on the department website. I'll email her."

"How will you get her to talk to you?"

"I'll tell her I'm transferring in and looking for a lab to join." She sighed. "And that I have law enforcement training, which often piques people's interest. I'll have to request credentials from the PBI."

"You don't have to do that."

"No, but this is important. I want you to be happy."

"And I want the same for you."

She gazed out the window. "I don't know if that's possible." Then she turned to her phone again—conversation over.

We drove the rest of the way to Atlanta in silence, and she disappeared into the guest suite she'd claimed as her room. I had happily offered her a place to stay as long as she needed, and I also acknowledged—with a side helping of guilt—that I counted down the days until she moved to Athens. I'd be free to join Reine in Scotland, or wherever I could when she was in this realm. We hadn't discussed it, but she'd made it reluctantly clear that when she assumed her full role as queen, she would have to spend more time there than here.

I poured an Irish whiskey and added an ice cube, then walked out to the porch. The late afternoon sun slanted through the trees in golden summer stripes. One of them hit a still gray form on the floor.

"Raleigh?" Recognition jolted through me and rattled the ice cube. I put the drink down and approached the grimalkin, who lay cold and still. "Shit!" The rare expletive escaped me, but several aspects of the situation warranted it. One, why was he here without Reine? Two, what was wrong with him? I recalled the first time I'd seen him like this was as a kitten who'd just made a big journey on his own. Third, one of his front legs, the one with the white paw, lay crooked. What could have damaged a tough supernatural creature to the point it had broken a leg?

I dashed to retrieve my stethoscope, and the sounds of faint breathing and a slow heartbeat sent cautious relief to my gut.

"Kestrel!"

"Yes?" She ran in, and her eyes widened. "Is that Sir Raleigh?" Although she didn't like Reine for valid reasons, she cared for the catlike grimalkin. "Is he okay?"

"No, his leg is broken. Please help me move him to a carrier so I can get him to..." Where? I couldn't get to my CPDC lab; it was on a different floor from the main office, but I suspected Cimex had disabled my entry card.

"Do you have any friends who can help?"

I thought through a few. One, a colleague I'd met at a conference several years prior, came to mind. I typically avoided the local continuing education events so I wouldn't have to say too much about where I practiced. Typically, "Atlanta" sufficed for those not from the area, but this person had been in Seattle and had combined a family visit and seminar so her workplace would cover the cost of her travel. Finally, I'd had to tell her I worked for the government but couldn't say more. We'd shared a dinner and some laughs, and she'd wanted more once we returned to the city. I hadn't called or texted her, and I hadn't given her my number.

If this had been like the last time I'd found Sir Raleigh after a rough trip, I would have kept him warm, given him fluids, and let him revive, but I needed an x-ray of the leg. I also wanted someone who'd give me more freedom to treat him than I'd find at an emergency vet, since he wasn't an ordinary cat.

With some trepidation, I scrolled back through my Notes app, where I'd put Elise MacNamara's number, and called.

She picked up with, "Are you going to deliver my sesame chicken, or aren't you?"

Her greeting reminded me of one reason I hadn't followed up with her—I'd avoided strong women until Reine, whom I hadn't liked at first, either.

"Hey, Elise, no Chinese food here. This is Lawrence Gordon, from the Pacific Northwest Feline Treatment Convention?"

A long pause. Had she hung up on me? Sometimes it was hard to tell on cell phones, since they didn't kick you back to a dial tone.

"Lawrence. What a surprise."

Not a pleasant one, according to her flat tone. I almost gave up, but I looked at Sir Raleigh. I liked the little guy, and he might be my only clue to finding Reine. "Hey, I'm sorry to bug you, but I have an emergency, and I didn't have anyone else to call."

"I'm the only vet in town?"

"I work for the government, so I don't get out much in the community."

"That explains a lot about the government. What do you need?"

Good, she hadn't said no or clicked off. "I'm watching my girlfriend's cat, and he hurt his leg while I was out. I can treat him, but I need an x-ray, and my machine's down. Do you have one?"

I knew she did. We'd talked about it.

"Girlfriend, huh?" A deep sigh. "If you bring me dinner, I'll help you out. I think the Golden Dragon lost my order."

"One sesame chicken coming right up. I'll get my favorite restaurant to deliver something for both of us. White or brown rice?"

~

WHEN I ARRIVED at Elise's office, our food and a curious Elise waited for us. She had pulled her long dark hair into a messy bun, and she still wore her lab coat. Everyone had gone home before I'd gotten there, and I expressed my appreciation of her keeping the place open for us.

Elise ignored my thanks and used one brown sauce-covered fried chunk of chicken expertly held with chopsticks to motion to a door.

"X-ray's through there. Do you need help sedating the cat?" She walked over to peer inside the carrier. "Pretty boy," she cooed, but none of that softness came through for me when she asked, "What do you think happened to him?"

"No idea, and I don't need help, but thank you."

"Is he an old cat?"

"No, he's young."

"It's too bad they can't tell us their family history, isn't it?"

"Definitely." I'd love to know what Raleigh would say to that. He'd been in and out of consciousness, and he hadn't communicated anything to me other than pain and worry, which made my stomach knot with nausea every time. The thought of the beef and broccoli I'd ordered didn't help.

"I'll put the films in for you."

She disappeared behind the tall white machine that was big enough to hold large dogs. Sir Raleigh looked tiny on the table. He lifted his head and glared at me through slitted eyes that spoke of betrayal. I couldn't tell whether it was for subjecting him to an unfamiliar place, and a vet's office to boot, or for interacting with a beautiful woman who wasn't Reine.

"I'm trying to help you," I told him. "Please don't disappear or do anything else that will create more questions."

He closed his eyes and laid his head down, and I again placed a hand on him to make sure he breathed.

Elise took the films with the same efficiency she did everything, and we both examined the leg. Sir Raleigh hadn't moved, but I felt him listening.

"Looks like a compression fracture, like he fell from a high place. Could he have been on your roof?"

"Not that I'm aware of."

"If you comfort him, I'll splint it for you."

I held Sir Raleigh against me. She fitted a splint on his leg and gave him a shot of pain medicine.

We settled into her staff break room, and Sir Raleigh lay on my lap while I ate. "Thank you," I told her. "I know I said I'd call and didn't..."

"And I was disappointed you didn't, but after a while, I figured it was for the best. Like, maybe you had a wife at home you hadn't told me about or something."

"No, nothing like that. I've just always been a loner." Being with Reine had shown me just how much of one I'd become. "And I didn't start dating my girlfriend until after I'd met you, so it wasn't that."

She laughed. "I knew you'd hate being the subject of suspicion. Don't worry, I could tell you've got a strong moral code. Thanks for dinner, by the way."

"You're welcome. It's the least I could do. And I'll pay for the x-ray and the rest of it."

My phone buzzed with a text, and I looked down to see a preview of something from Kestrel. *Heard back from grd...*

"Do you mind?" I asked. "It's important."

"Not at all." She stood. "I'm going to take care of some paperwork. Take your time."

I unlocked the phone and read, *Heard back fr grd stdnt. In town tonight. Meeting 4 drinks. 30 min at corner bar near your place.*

Will try to come. Still at other vet's.

How is cat?

Resting. Compression fracture.

Poor kitty!

I scratched Raleigh behind the ears, and he purred slightly, so I knew he was at least somewhat conscious. *"We should head out, shouldn't we?"* I asked him in what Reine called "secret conversation," the Fae term for telepathy. He'd talked to me on rare occasions, and indeed, he favored me with a brief response, although it didn't comfort me.

"Reine lost. Can't find her."

"What happened?" I asked out loud.

"Long fall. Hurt. Ellerin lost. Reine lost." Then he lapsed back into sleep. I pieced together what he'd said or tried to. It made sense he'd gone to Ellerin, presumably in Faerie, for help first. But what could the long fall have been? Reine had texted me from Scotland, so I knew her plane hadn't crashed. Some other sort of accident?

I pulled out my phone, but Elise returned before I could look up plane tickets to Scotland.

"Yes?" I asked.

"Look, I had another reason for agreeing to help your girl-friend's cat." She nodded to him. "His isn't the first injury I've seen like that, and the owners have no clue what happened."

"You mean, other unexplained cat injuries?" Regular cats couldn't have developed the ability to teleport, could they? No, impossible.

"Yeah. Like something scared them so badly they ran in a blind panic. One or two, I could dismiss. But this is the fifth this week."

I couldn't tell her my theory behind Sir Raleigh's injury, but he wasn't an ordinary case. "How many have you seen total?"

"I'd have to sit down and count them, but enough to stand out. At first, I thought I'd have to report for abuse, but this is a pattern." She scratched Raleigh behind the ears, and I caught the light scent of her perfume. I cleared my throat, and she moved back.

"Thank you for telling me."

"You never said exactly what your fancy government job was, but it seemed like something you should know. I'd been putting off contacting you because, you know..."

"Yes, sorry again. I wasn't in a place to think about dating."

She glanced up through her dark lashes. "And some lucky woman got a hold of you before I could."

I couldn't help the smile that emerged at the memory of the warmth that came with holding Reine, like a ray of sunshine through a cloud of worry. "Yes, she's special." And in danger. "Thanks for letting me know. I'll see what else has been reported. And it's only been cats?"

"A few dogs, but mostly cats. Something's putting these animals into a flee state." She shook her head. "That's why I'm here so late. Had to do an emergency surgery on one animal. She'll be okay, but..."

"I understand. It's hard to see preventable injuries, or at least ones that should be preventable."

We said our goodbyes, and I tucked Sir Raleigh into his carrier. I glanced back one more time to check on him, and he opened his eyes fully and looked at me through the door.

"You were playing possum, weren't you?"

A bob of the head that could have been a nod.

"And what do you think about these animals that are being hurt?"

He laid his head down, and his ears twitched. I took that as a sign he didn't know.

"Yeah, another mystery, like what happened to your mum."

"Mrrrowl." The sound carried the same weight as the lump of sorrow and worry in my chest.

"We'll figure it out. I'm going to meet up with Kestrel. I'll drop you on the way."

He vanished, which I took to mean he would meet me at my place. I shook my head and started the car. What would Elise think of a teleporting cat? I wouldn't tell her, but the thought of her reaction gave me some amusement. Until this point, it had felt like Reine was the one being targeted, but finding out about the animals...now it felt personal, assuming what occurred had a supernatural origin.

Until a few months before, I would have dismissed the thought, but no longer. When one dealt with the Fae, anything was possible, including the one I loved being in danger.

My phone rang, and I glanced down to see my mother's name.

13

REINE

When Lonna and I walked over to investigate the source of the chuckle, we found no one, but two footprints indented the soft soil between the shrubs. They looked to be from men's boots.

"Not modern shoes," Lonna observed. "No pattern on the soles, at least not what you'd expect from a modern factory."

"That makes it even stranger."

She slid me a sly glance. "That's something coming from you."

I didn't sense an insult, so I sighed. "That seems to be the order of the day."

We turned and walked back toward the cottage under the brightening sky. With the golden light pouring through the windows, the place looked like a painting from a fairy tale.

Lonna rubbed her eyes, and I recalled she hadn't slept in a day. "What are you going to do?"

"I had a strange dream when I napped earlier. Yesterday. I suspect it wasn't a dream, so I'm going to attempt something similar and reach out to my contacts in Faerie. It's time for a check-in anyway." I'd promised my Council of Three that I'd be in touch a couple of times a week to get updates on the revenant situation and others.

"And what about us?"

"Get some sleep. It's been a long day and night, and exposure to that much magical energy can be exhausting."

We walked in to find Selene sitting alone with Lonna's phone in her hand. "They vanished."

"It must be dawn, then, or close to it." Had that been what happened to our watcher in the woods, also vanished at dawn? Who was he? I'd have to trap him the next night.

Lonna held out her hand to Selene. "You're exhausted, as am I. Let's try to sleep. We'll think clearer for it."

Selene gave her the phone and stood. "I know. But I'm worried. About everything."

"Me, too. Reine, are you all right out here?"

"Yes, I'll figure something out. Perhaps I'll sleep outside, get the energy of the earth to help me."

They walked into the bedroom, leaving me in the main room. I straightened up, although I expected that come dusk, it would return to how it had been when Irina and Meg had appeared. Indeed, the more the sunlight filled the room, the more it decayed. I sat and pondered my options. Sure, I wanted to reach out to Troubadour, but I feared I'd fail. What if we were stuck here forever, doomed to eventually disappear at dawn and reappear at dusk? How would the lycanthropes handle it? Would they ever need to change under the false moon?

I walked outside and wandered around the overgrown and fallow garden. An unusually green grassy spot invited me to take my shoes off, and I wriggled my toes in the soft thatch. The earth felt different here, almost like it had been disconnected, which confirmed the theory that the cottage and land around it stood in a place outside of the normal flow of time, an orthogonal dimension. How had our appearance there changed the spell, if at all? Another mystery to ponder.

I folded my legs under me to sit on the grass and gazed around. Then I put my head on my knees and wrapped my arms around my shins, and after a few deep breaths, the darkness in the periphery of my visual field spread, and I slipped into slumber.

A BREEZE STIRRED MY HAIR, and I lifted my gaze to the gardens of the palace of the light Fae. I stood and found I wore a long robe of light blue and silver, and I touched the platinum circlet at my forehead, signifying my queendom to be once I returned to Faerie to claim it. Although I moved in a dream body, the metal band pressed into my skin.

How long would my journey last? I couldn't say, so I moved toward the palace itself and found myself in the throne room without having to go inside or walk through all the halls. The throne stood empty. None of the Council of Three would dare sit in it, although Basil, whom I'd first known as Troubadour, probably wouldn't mind the consort throne. He thought he hid his hope that I'd come around and align myself romantically with a Fae, but a certain gargoyle held my heart.

Lawrence... I hadn't allowed myself to think of him, how he must be worried sick about me. I'd seen the wistful expressions on Lonna's and Selene's faces, and I knew they wanted to move on with our mission of helping to find Gabriel and Max as much as I craved being in Lawrence's presence. I hoped he stayed safe, especially after his mother's warning. At least he had Kestrel to keep him busy. Although she hadn't yet figured out how to control her magic with any consistency, she might offer him some protection.

My next blink took me to the library, where I found Basil

head-down in the midst of piles of books and scrolls. His soft snore vibrated through my middle and stirred up the dregs of guilt about how hard he worked as part of the Council of Three, especially since Ellerin had vanished. I didn't delude myself into thinking that my brother Rhys, the third on the council, would pick up the slack.

A map of Faerie took up the entirety of one of the large square tables. Something appeared off, so I leaned over it and traced the boundaries of the Gray Zone, the buffer between the Light and Dark Fae lands.

"Has it gotten larger?" I murmured.

Warmth at my shoulder made me twist to see a now-awake Basil beside me. "The Winter Goblin King alerted us to its spread. I've been trying to keep up with it, but it doesn't have a pattern and sometimes recedes."

"What do you think it means?"

He ran a hand through his thick blond hair and gave me his typical rueful grin. "What does it matter without our queen here to lead us? Are you coming to me as a ghost yourself to tell me you've decided to follow Ellerin undercover?"

"No, and is that what he's doing? He should have told me."

"In truth, I don't know."

I pushed the circlet up and rubbed where it had started to chafe. "I don't know how much time I have, so please listen. I'm caught in some sort of time loop along with Lonna Marconi, the head of the Institute for Lycanthropic Reversal, and Selene Rial, who works there and has been a co-adventurer." I didn't know that I could call her a friend. We hadn't gotten along, mostly due to my Fae attitude.

He crossed his arms. "What happened to make you fall into a rookie trap like that?"

I couldn't be mad at him. I'd been asking myself the same question.

I rolled my eyes. "It shouldn't have trapped me. It was my

spell to begin with, a protection spell so that only those with good intentions could find the witch who lived in the cottage. She'd done a favor for me, and it was around the time of Culloden, so I didn't want any harm to come to her."

"I see." He picked up a quill and tapped his lips with the end of the feather.

"Please tell me you have better writing implements than that."

"Your grandmother didn't upgrade. Don't worry, I've modified it, so I don't have to keep filling it. But you're saying that somehow your spell got turned inside out, and you're stuck."

"That's one way of looking at it. And the fireplace showed us all a scene from my life, back in the late seventeen hundreds. Another witch I helped." And changed the course of her life, but since I didn't know exactly how, I didn't say anything.

"So you're saying that you're trapped in one witch's cottage, and you saw a scene with another one. Is anyone else there?"

I explained about Irina and little Meg, who was the only clue I had to how time had passed for them. Would they appear the following night, or would it be another year?

"I can't say." Basil scribbled notes. "That time loop business gets tricky, as you know."

I found myself sad at the thought of not seeing them again, and then something else occurred to me. "There's also someone watching. Some guy. I heard his chuckle and found his footprints, but he'd vanished."

"This gets creepier by the second, Highness."

"You're not wrong. So that's my situation. What's the update here?"

"Reports of revenants have increased, the borders of the Gray Zone are shifting, and you already know about Ellerin."

"What have you heard from our other allies? And have you had any luck getting the dark Fae queen to talk to you about the revenant issue?"

"We're still going through the diplomatic channels. She is apparently displeased that I'm here helping you. She says we have plenty of old dusty scrolls and sneeze-inducing leather books in the library in Cruaidh."

I placed a hand on his arm, and I could see the royal blue velvet fabric of his sleeves through my fingers. "Hades, it must be time to go. I appreciate all your hard work. Please let me know what I can do to help."

"From your stuck position? Not much." He tapped his lips again. "I'll continue to noodle on your predicament, but something occurred to me." He held up a finger, and a book flew to him. He caught it, and it fell open in his palms. "Ah, yes, protection spells. Should gradually fade after a human lifetime unless something else interferes with it."

Chills danced across my neck and arms. "What sort of something else?"

"The spell of another Fae, one with ability similar to yours."

I wanted to ask him what that meant—didn't we all have the same sort of magic beyond slight variation in elemental ability?—but the library faded, and I found myself lying on my side.

I opened my eyes to on the patch of grass, which had gone brown, the shadows cast by the sun, which had dipped behind the trees, and the scuffed toes of two large, booted feet.

14

LAWRENCE

Since I was driving, I let my mother's call go to voice mail. When I arrived at the Shaded Tavern, I put the now-empty carrier into the trunk so no erstwhile good Samaritans would break a window to rescue an animal that wasn't there. I was actually relieved that Sir Raleigh had decided to teleport back to my place, or wherever he'd decided to go. Although I knew he wasn't a typical cat, I found his behavior consistent with feline attitude, which meant he might or might not show appreciation for my attempts to help him. At least he'd taken the splint.

I found Kestrel at a booth sitting across from a young woman whose long dark hair hung in loose waves, so I couldn't see her face. Kestrel waved at me, and the other girl turned. When my gaze met her dark green eyes, I identified her species, and recognition jolted me to my toes.

What was a dark Fae doing working with a dimension-walker?

"Well met," I said and slid into the booth beside Kestrel.

Kestrel darted a confused look between us. "Wait, you know her?"

"No, but I know what she is."

"My *name* is Lily," the student said and motioned with her palm down. "And had I known I'd be meeting with one of *you*, I would have declined."

"Wait, what's happening?"

I leaned over and whispered in Kestrel's ear, "Use your glamour-stripping power." She closed her eyes and scrunched her brows, and then when she opened them, they widened, and she said, "Ohhhh... This just gets weirder."

The waitress came over, took my order, and handed the girls their drinks.

"I'll take my check, too," Lily said.

"Is everything okay, hon?" The server shot me a dirty look. I could only imagine how we appeared.

"Yes, thank you. I just need to go. Soon."

When the server walked away, I took a deep breath so I could dispel some of the hostility, both in my own gut and floating around me. "I'm sorry, I didn't mean to seem like we were ambushing you. I was glad Kestrel got in touch with you because I, ah, need your help."

She arched one eyebrow, delicate and dark as a raven's feather. "You need my help? You mean, as in more than hooking this one up with a research position in our lab."

Kestrel broke in. "That, too. Like I was telling you, I'm eager to be a normal student for a while."

"And let me guess, that special training program you were in—that was the PBI, wasn't it?"

Kestrel's cheeks turned pink, and she studied her vodka tonic. "I can't say."

The server brought Lily's check, and I grabbed it. "I'll take care of this."

Lily swiped at it, but I held it away from her. "You don't have to, really." Panic tinted her voice.

"It's fine." I passed the bill along with a twenty to the server. "Keep the change."

"Well-played, Stoney," she said. "I'm now in your debt. Can I at least get your name?"

"Lawrence Gordon. Doctor Lawrence Gordon."

She cocked her head, and my entire skull tingled for a second. "Nope, can't use that against you. You're bonded with another Fae, and royalty at that." She let out a low whistle. "That's intriguing. What game are you playing?"

Maybe being with Reine had made me more sensitive to the layers of Fae trickery and subtle communication. "I'm wondering the same, since you so obviously don't want to make a scene. Why haven't you stormed out of here yet?"

She shrugged and sipped at her white wine. "As satisfying as that may be, it wouldn't be worth the consequences."

"You don't want to draw attention to yourself," Kestrel said.

"Yep, must be PBI. And you're correct. I've got more going on than you two could ever know. So again, what do you want?"

Although we had her at more than one disadvantage, she regarded us as though we owed her something. Typical Fae. Who was she, really? I wanted to pull my phone out and text Reine, but that reminded me—she was currently trapped somewhere.

"We have a friend in trouble," I told her.

"Your Fae girlfriend, I presume."

I reminded myself I couldn't trust a Fae, so I decided to stick with what we'd originally planned to ask her to do. "Possibly. But the original reason for our approaching you was that we need Doctor Grand-Pied's help with a very old problem in Faerie."

"What could he possibly—oh, I get it. You need a powerful Earth and Air elemental to do a spell to make Faerie's air breathable for you, is that it?"

Kestrel narrowed her eyes. "You put that together quickly. Too quickly."

Lily shrugged. "Word gets around, especially of a certain Fae who went to The Aerie and got rid of an ice witch. A powerful ice witch who refused to help her with that same problem. Is that correct, Doctor Stoney?"

I suppressed a groan at the evidence that somehow the news had gotten out and had been twisted. I knew from my own previous prejudice that I would have easily believed the worst-looking scenario for the Fae. "As tends to happen with gossip, some of the aspects of the situation are correct, but the details are wrong. The ice witch perished as a result of a self-defense move by one of our party."

I recognized my slip as soon as I said it, and she pounced on it. "'By one of your party.' Meaning you were there. You're the gargoyle that the Fae wants to bring back to Faerie with her."

I caught myself rubbing my chest. The memory of the suffocating sensation felt like it bruised me internally every time, especially when the mate bond's ache joined in. "I can't say any more. But do you think he'll help us if we can convince him?"

"And you need me to help you get close to him." She swirled her wine. "Let me guess, you've tried, and he blew you off."

"Yes," both Kestrel and I said. I added, "He told us to leave him alone. And for her to take the intermediate class."

Lily's red lips tucked into a smirk. "That sounds about right. Why do you think we don't have any undergraduate help? He chases them all off."

"So you do need help," Kestrel said.

"We have mountains of data that needs to be coded, and I don't have time to sit there and do it. But he refuses to let anyone into our lab." She stopped swirling and sipped. "What if I offer you a bargain?"

We both sat straight like someone had shocked us. "No bargains," I growled.

Lily laughed. "Not like that. Let's say you convince Grand-Pied to take on a student, the trickster here, and I'll nudge him in the direction of helping you with the gargoyle problem."

"What do you mean by nudge?"

She shrugged. "He's my advisor. I can't make him do anything, but I know how to appeal to his curiosity. He pretends he doesn't, but he likes big problems, and changing an entire dimension's atmosphere sounds like the biggest challenge of all."

"Thank you," Kestrel said. "I'm willing to do what I can to help. For my own academic career," she added.

I didn't comment, although I heard plenty of what she'd left unsaid. What would it mean if we fixed the atmosphere in Faerie? Would I move there? I guessed she didn't want me to leave her forever. Nor did I intend to. I'd figure out a balance like Reine would have to. Just as Reine had her obligations, I had mine.

Lily might have had some of the Fae ability to read minds, or at least feelings. "And what about your friend? Now that we've been telling secrets."

I studied my own drink, which the server had just delivered. Irish whiskey rather than Scotch, which was fine. "I don't know, and that's the problem."

She smirked. "Now I definitely know you're involved with..." She pointed a thumb toward her breastbone. "One of us."

"As if you needed the confirmation," Kestrel mumbled.

"No, she's disappeared, and I can't get in touch with her."

"Are you sure she hasn't decided to move on to someone else? We do that, you know. We're not exactly known for our loyalty."

"I'm sure. I've had other evidence that she's in trouble. Clear evidence."

"Hmmm…" She tilted her head again. "Yes, I sense your concern is true and founded. Who is your friend? I may be able to help."

Kestrel and I exchanged a look, and she shrugged. "Your call, Uncle."

Since I'd run out of ideas beyond dashing to Scotland and looking for her myself, which probably wouldn't do any good since Fae typically didn't help gargoyles, and I had no leads whatsoever, I decided to tell her. "Reine."

Lily spat out the wine she'd just sipped. "Reine. As in Princess Reine in line for the light throne Reine?"

Kestrel grinned. "You must've been gone for a while. She's now the queen of the light Fae."

"How? Maeve would never stand for that. Iron and bones, this complicates things. You have to fill me in. Right now." She glanced over my shoulder, gulped air, then said, "Never mind. I'm not part of that world anymore. I'm sorry, I can't help you with your friend. And don't give her my regards if you see her."

She tossed a couple of dollars on the table. "For a tip. Email me about the professor." With that, she slipped out of our booth and disappeared into the growing crowd around the bar, which stood between us and the exit.

"That was strange," I observed.

"Yes." Kestrel had twisted around. She returned to facing the table. "I couldn't see what spooked her, but something did."

I paid the rest of the tab, and we walked out to the car in the twilight. I thought I saw an extra shadow, and indeed, Sir Raleigh appeared on Kestrel's lap once she'd gotten settled and put on her seatbelt. He still wore the splint.

"Hey, Raleigh," she said and scratched him behind the ears.

He shot me a look that plainly said, "You'd better be making progress," before curling up and purring. I didn't begrudge him his comfort. I wished I had someone who would do that for me, but the problem was, the only person I wanted to was in the trouble that made me need soothing.

I pulled out on to the road, which was clogged with evening traffic. A dark blue Camry pulled out after me, and with the angle of the setting sun, I couldn't see the driver's face, only that they had a halo of thick hair. Another dimension-walker?

I shook my head, but was it paranoia if something really was following me? I opted to turn right at the next cross street rather than left to go into my neighborhood. Instead of going straight, which led into town, the Camry turned right after me into a different subdivision.

"What are you doing?" Kestrel asked.

"Don't turn around. I think we're being followed." Sure, they could live there, but I looped through the silent streets and back out to the road. For a second, I thought they'd turned into one of the driveways, but then I noticed them hanging back. "Hades," I said, borrowing Reine's favorite expletive. "Someone's tailing us."

15

REINE

Some old bit of Fae training kicked in, and I called upon my ice lasso again—cue the Elsa comparisons—and caught the guy around one ankle. He turned and ran, and I managed to scramble to my feet.

"Hades! Stop, I just want to talk to you."

All I could see was the back of his head, which had longish salt and pepper curly hair, not his face. His stocky, muscular build filled out the wide-sleeved shirt and leather jerkin, and he wore breeches of some sort of thick material, which were tucked into the boots I'd noticed. I placed his time period in the eighteenth century.

And he was strong. I barely kept my feet as my lasso dragged me along behind him. He headed into the woods and straight to the time bubble barrier. Then he ran through it. My lasso remained taut, and I held on and braced myself for impact or to be turned around. But neither happened. I passed through an electric curtain that left all my hair standing on end and skidded to a stop on the other side. My lasso, now just an ordinary rope, hung loose in my hand. I gathered it and found the end frayed.

What sort of magic could have done that? The transformation of energy to plain rope definitely spoke of Fae power, and someone not afraid to arouse suspicion about our transmogrification abilities.

A splash caught my attention, and my focus snapped from the rope to my environment. I stood in an alley between two stone buildings. Their orange tile roofs blocked out much of the watery sunlight filtered through heavy clouds. The splash had been made by a startled cat that at first I hoped was Sir Raleigh, but no, this one had orange stripes and slunk away.

"Hades," I muttered again. "Where in the realms am I?"

I attached the rope to a hook on my belt, and upon looking down, found I wore a simple blue dress and the same long gray cloak I'd had on in the fireplace vision. Sturdy boots encased my feet, and the pouch at my belt lay full of coins.

Had I been dragged into one of my memories? That didn't make sense, but I decided to follow my instincts and see if I could place when and where I'd landed.

Once I set the intention, my legs and feet started walking, and I allowed myself to be pulled wherever this journey led. Once I emerged on to a main thoroughfare, I recognized the place—Prague in the 1850s. This would be another failed mission to seek help for Rhys. So why had I come here? I sensed I'd find a clue to releasing myself from the time bubble, but how much would I actively have to seek it? Would I need to ask a certain question, or simply notice something? If I'd been a heroine in a fairy tale, I would have automatically known, but as a Fae, I didn't have the sort of human compulsion the old tales built into their protagonists.

I turned and took in as much of the city as I could, especially the people. Even at that time, Prague had been a bustling, diverse place, and I caught features, clothing, and languages from all over the world. I also noticed many of the old symbols that had once been so common as to be invisible, but now stood out to me, as accustomed as I'd become to modern architecture.

The memory came back to me more clearly, and so I wasn't surprised when I stopped in front of a small shop near the Charles Bridge. It belonged to an alchemist, who also treated paranormal beings. An old vampire, he'd originally been part of the Knights Hospitaller during the Crusades and then had been turned. He hated what he'd become and so focused his attention on healing those who couldn't find help elsewhere. I'd heard of him through my network of witches and alchemists in England since he supplied many of them with herbs that could only be found on the continent. He'd been mail delivery for plants before that had become a thing. He wouldn't be awake until nightfall, so I whispered a spell and felt the rope tug me in a direction perpendicular to where I came.

"I'd be careful if I were you, witch," came a voice from behind me. I whirled around to see a man dressed as a minor noble, but his costume didn't fit his bearing. He held himself like a soldier with one hand on his sword hilt, and the other on his waist, where I had no doubt some sort of firearm lay hidden.

"I'm not a witch." Not a lie—I wasn't.

"Ah, I see now. You're one of the nature walkers."

Even if I could have lied, I wouldn't have. I didn't remember this interaction, and I didn't want to make too many waves being here. Would he forget me once I left?

"In a sense, yes, although I've wandered far from home."

"Did you come from the river, then?" He had light blue eyes with wrinkles beside them, and I caught a hint of sandy brown hair under his tall felt hat.

"No, from the country. And if you'll excuse me, I have a man to find."

"Not the one who lives there, I hope. He's been gone for several weeks."

I turned back to him. If that was the case, I hadn't landed in a memory. So where, or more appropriately, when, in Hades was I? And how did I get back to my own time and not in the bubble?

"Do you know where he went?"

"No." Just that. No explanation or further questions, which immediately made me suspicious.

"Do you know *when* he went?" Sure, it was a long shot, but disoriented didn't even begin to describe how I felt.

"I'm not sure the meaning of that query, milady. But he vanished soon after one like you visited him."

I cast back through the murk of memory, which was almost two hundred years previously, to think of when I'd seen the alchemist and what had happened.

He stepped closer and lowered his voice. "There are some who say he wasn't human, and that his only coming out at night wasn't due to his weak eyesight and skin condition that not even he, the most talented alchemist among us, could cure."

I tried to determine what sort of creature stood in front of me, but he'd managed to mask his aura. "So you're an alchemist as well?"

He nodded.

I put together his posture and general air of readiness. "You're a Hospitaller."

"Milady!" He glanced around. "Surely you know that order has been disbanded for many a hundred-year now."

"Yeah, like the Templars." I didn't hide the bitterness in my tone. Although Rhys had been healed, one of my grandmother's final actions, I still hated the order whose member had contributed to his mutilation and my long exile.

He smirked. "I should know better than to try to fool one whose memory is as long as yours. And now that you know that it is my task to guard this fair city as well as to ply my healing trade, who, may I ask, are you to come here and cause mischief with your magic making?"

I didn't back down even though he stood closer than my personal level of comfort allowed. I'd spent too much time among the Americans with their desire for more personal space than anyone else on the globe. In fact, I drew myself up to my full height and matched his haughty manner.

"I am one of the high nature walkers, and you should know that interfering with my efforts could end badly for you, good sir."

"And you know that the laws do not allow magic to be performed outside of healing and alchemy."

That explained part of the rope turning from magical to mundane, but it would still require a spell to make it do so. Who had the leaders of the city allied with? "Perhaps you would grant an exception to one such as I, then, as I hunt a fugitive. I had almost captured him, but he slipped away."

"What does he look like?"

I described what I'd seen.

"And his face?"

"I didn't see it."

Confusion, then exasperation marched across his face. "You're telling me, fair walker, that this person woke you from a nap, and you decided to punish him, but couldn't capture him when he ran away."

"No one disturbs a nature walker's nap. And it was more than that. He's been watching me threateningly and menacing me and my companions."

A young boy ran up to the man, who hadn't given me his name. I understood and mentally applauded his caution, but sometimes it made communication damn difficult. The boy whispered in his ear.

"And would your companions be a redhead and a brunette, both exceedingly tall like you?"

Oh, Hades, had Selene and Lonna managed to follow me?

"Perhaps."

"Then come with me. I have questions for all of you."

I FOLLOWED the caped man through the streets. People leaped out of his way, which told me more about him than he could have described. They respected and feared him, so he must take his role as a guard more seriously than his healing arts.

The old me would have found him to be a challenge. His face had a rugged handsomeness to it I found attractive, and the stuffier a human—or paranormal—the more fun they were to break down. I'd left a trail of broken spirits behind me. Someone like him would question where he'd gone weak to allow a Fae to seduce him and then leave him craving her for the rest of his life. I thought it was fun at the time, but at some point, the strange human emotion of guilt had started catching up with me, and I'd become a hermit. And then I'd met Lawrence.

Lawrence... I rubbed the bone over the spot in my chest that continually ached to be with him, my forbidden mate and impossible match. At least the pain told me I hadn't been completely sucked into this time period. I sensed I needed to figure out what had happened to Bartholemew, the alchemist who had given me a salve that hadn't worked. Why had he left after my visit? I'd helped him because he'd developed a rare case of vampirepox, which only infected one every thousand years, and I'd healed him. Had I done something wrong? Made a mistake and caused his illness to grow worse? Again, it was difficult to think back and remember exactly because so much had gone on since that time. But if he had succumbed, he would have eventually gone poof like a vampire who hit the sunlight.

My guide brought me to a castle that was old by even the standards of that time. The two symbols of the Hospitallers and Templars, a black Maltese Cross and red cross on white background, had been carved over the door. We entered, and I pulled my cloak closer against the cold. I recalled now I'd visited the old vampire healer close to the autumn equinox, and they'd been having an unseasonably warm fall. The inside of the castle felt like full winter, and not even the fire in the great hall fireplace dispelled the chill.

"They don't make these like they used to," I muttered.

"Make what?"

"Castles. Get some tapestries or something. It's bone chilling cold in here."

He allowed himself a rueful grin. "I'm afraid it's something about the walls, Milady. But come with me. Your friends are upstairs."

I followed him up a narrow flight of stairs and through a hallway lined with portraits of commanders and generals and other men with titles that would sound important to humans. The chill continued, although the stuffiness abated somewhat on the second floor. I walked as far away as possible from the iron weapons that hung on the walls. They buzzed with *wrongness.*

He brought me to a large office-looking space, where two men guarded Lonna and Selene, both of whom glared at their captors, and neither of whom seemed happy to see me. Ungrateful wenches. They each wore long simple dresses, cloaks, and bonnets.

"Are these them?" he asked.

"Yes, let them go."

"You heard the lady, soldiers. Untie them." He motioned to the two men who flanked Selene and Lonna. Soon his orders had been followed, and they rubbed their newly untied wrists.

"There you are!" Lonna moved to approach me, but the man beside her lowered his axe in front of her.

"What is the meaning of this?" I asked and turned toward the commander. "We haven't done anything wrong, so you have no grounds to hold us."

He pushed the cloak back from his shoulder, and a small silver pin that sat above his left pectoral in the shape of an arrow told me I'd walked into a trap.

16

REINE

"I believe I see why Bartholomew de Veers disappeared," I said. "You had a hand in that, didn't you?"

"He may have had some help, but it wasn't from me, Milady. Please, have a seat."

With a huff, I sat beside Selene on a cushioned fainting couch. Thankfully bustles hadn't come into fashion yet, and we wore narrow everyday skirts. How had we ended up in period appropriate dress? Had that been part of the trap?

And had the man who creepily watched me sleep been part of it?

"Fine, what do you want?" I mimed checking my wristwatch, then remembered he wouldn't know that that meant. "We don't have all day." All right, technically we had almost two hundred years, but I wasn't going to say that. He didn't seem to recognize that we came from a different time period, so we had that to our advantage. As for changing history... I didn't know what to do aside from get out as soon as possible.

"Would you ladies like something to eat? To drink? I wouldn't want you to return to your realm complaining of our hospitality."

The three of us exchanged looks, and I could almost hear their agreement. *No way, it may be drugged.*

"No, thank you. Ask your questions and let us be on our way." I made a little flame dance above my right palm. "Otherwise, my little friend here may get frisky with all those lovely antique books."

"Many of them are recent printings, but I get your point. I've been watching Herr de Veers' shop for several weeks in hopes he'd return, and you're the first odd person to appear. Therefore, you are under suspicion of assisting in his disappearance."

"I can assure you I did no such thing. I've been in the United States for the past several weeks and have only journeyed back to Europe recently." All technically true...

"You said you were in the country."

"Where I went before I came into the city. I'm not obligated to give you my entire itinerary."

The little flame lengthened, and I took a deep breath so my frustration wouldn't interfere with my good sense. I could smite our captors, but again, I couldn't risk the potential fallout of doing big spells in the middle of a time loop. Although we'd stepped out of it, its magic still held us.

"Still... Would you prefer that we torture your friends so they tell us the truth?"

"We don't know anything!" Selene objected. Then she turned to me. "Reine, I'm not feeling well." The look she gave me told me what she meant—a full moon must be nigh, along with the urge to transform.

Oh, Hades. If she changed, these three from the Order of the Silver Arrow, the secret society notorious for slaughtering shifters, would kill them. They'd know to attack in that vulnerable moment mid-shift when they'd be defenseless.

I stood. "It's all right. We'll be out of here soon. We really must be going, gentlemen. Do you have any other questions?"

The leader checked his pocket watch. "It's almost dinner

time. I insist that you accept our hospitality. Then I'll figure out what to do with you. Henric, stand guard outside the door. Don't let anyone in or out. Someone will bring food in for you soon."

The three men left, and Lonna jumped to her feet. "Reine, we need to go. Once the sun goes down and the moon comes up, we're going to wolf out."

"Hades." I looked around. We were in some sort of library, and a dusty cabinet in the corner caught my attention. "Wait, there may be a solution here. Have either of you spirit-walked? Lonna, you have, right?"

"Yes, although my inner wolf doesn't like it."

"Let me see what I can find." I walked over to the cabinet, praying that my Latin wouldn't fail me. I hoped that Wolfsbane, or aconite, would be on the shelves and that I would recognize what it had been called back in the olden days if not by one of those names.

The herbs in the jars had disintegrated to dusty gray fragments, so I doubted any would be usable.

"Sunset, Reine," Lonna called from the window. I'd never heard that shrill degree of panic her voice before. Would I soon be confronted with a couple of snarling wolves I'd then have to defend myself against and protect? I knew nothing of how a time loop would affect their awareness of me. Would they become confused and aggressive?

"Hades. How did the two of you even get here?"

Selene lifted her head from her hands. She'd been sitting with elbows on knees and bent over, likely trying to hold herself together. "We saw you get dragged through the barrier and followed you. We hoped you'd found a way out. I certainly didn't expect this."

"And how did you get picked up?" I grabbed the jar with the most intact fragments. It wasn't aconite, but I remembered enough of the chemical signature to transform it—I hoped.

Lonna replied, "Two soldiers saw us wandering over the bridge and trying to decipher the sign to figure out where we were. They made rude overtures toward us, and, uh, I may have told them exactly where they could stick their wandering hands."

"Did they hurt you?" So help me goddess, I would smite those bastards, and time bubble consequences be damned.

"No, not at all," Selene said with a rueful smile. "But they got the message we're not from around here."

"All right, I think this will do." I focused on changing some of the mint leaves I'd found into aconite using the Fae ability to transmogrify things. I gambled that such a small change wouldn't cause any sort of major consequence, but I still held my breath for a few seconds after I completed the job. Nothing happened, so I pulled open the glass lid and handed each of them a leaf.

"When you feel the urge to change, put these under your tongues and try not to chew. I don't know how strong they are."

"And then where do we go? I don't know how solid I'll be."

"Hide." I handed over the leaves, but they dropped through their hands as they became more transparent. I looked down to see the floor through my own skirt. With a rushing sound, we ended up back in the cottage with lights blazing but no Irina and Meg.

And two snarling wolves who looked at me like I would make a perfect snack. I blinked to clear the burning image of a sideways Y from my vision and backed up.

BOTH WOLVES GLOWED, which indicated they still hung on to the moon energy from our travels to Prague in eighteen-whatever-it-had-been. I wished I could remember more of the visit to Bartholemew de Veers. I'd healed the lesion that indicated he would decay into the vampire's long sleep soon. They didn't live forever, and they rarely died a natural death, so it was no wonder he, the greatest alchemist no one had ever heard of, hadn't known the signs of his impending doom. Perhaps he'd taken a final trip to say his goodbyes.

"*Luna, vaten,*" I whispered in the old tongue instead of English out of respect for Bartholemew and because I felt more connected to my past, even if the mists of long memory hid many of the details.

The two wolves shivered and returned to their human forms. Although they'd damaged their eighteenth-century clothing, their modern outfits lay in heaps on the floor. I walked into the bedroom to let them readjust to human brains and dress. This evening no skeletal intruder lay on the bed, and I suspected Irina and Meg didn't appear every day. Otherwise, Meg would have aged more. And I would have seen them on my rare visits back to the cottage, which I'd thought maintained its slow rate of decay due to my spell. I'd never thought to look otherwise. Judging from Meg's apparent age of four or five, they perhaps lived two days out of every year.

Although I hadn't been the one to trap them in the spell, the mantle of responsibility for their predicament settled over me. What would they do once I freed them? The Fae had resources to give foundlings, Fae exiles, and visitors to the Earth realm identification, but our reach only went so far. That had been another reason for me hiding out in my own cottage in my enchanted woods. Until my mother decided to get rid of me for good.

"Are you decent?" I called to the others. We Fae didn't do family relationships like humans, but if I thought about Maeve too hard, a strange ache formed under my sternum.

"Yes," came Lonna's weary reply. "You can come out now."

She and Selene had split the candy bar that Selene had

offered to Meg and that the girl had rejected because of its wrapper. Yes, those two would have a lot to become accustomed to in the modern world, like how we wrapped our food in potentially toxic materials.

"Do you want a bite?" Selene asked.

"No, thank you. I can go a long time between eating." And if I needed to, I'd transform something. "Are you two all right?"

They exchanged a look that spoke volumes of their exhaustion and flagging spirits. "As well as could be expected," was Lonna's response.

"What about you?" Selene pulled the chair beside her out and patted the cushion.

I accepted the seat but remained tense in case Lonna's sharp tongue made me want to smite her. "What about me? I'm as tired as the two of you, and as worried."

Lonna scoffed. "How could you possibly be as worried as we are? You don't have a husband or fiancé missing."

"As far as I know." Worry for Lawrence escaped the cage I'd put it in and crawled through my chest. "If your mates have been targeted, why wouldn't mine?"

Selene faced me and raised her eyebrows. "Lawrence Gordon is your mate now? That got serious quickly."

I studied the ancient pattern of scratches on the wood. Had Meg made them while practicing her letters? Or had Irina not been careful while slicing something? Each told the secret story of a domestic mishap, the kind I'd never have with Lawrence since he couldn't live in Faerie.

"We're working things out. Trying to. He has obligations." As did I. And sometimes all of them put tall obsidian walls between us.

Lonna didn't seem interested in my problems. "No one's going to solve anything while we're stuck here. Do you know where that was and why we got sucked there?"

"You mean when you followed me."

"We didn't want to lose you. We were concerned." Selene didn't say whether their concern was for me or themselves.

"And no, I don't. When I asked the spell to show me why we were stuck in a time loop, it showed me that first memory of me and Rhys going to the witch to see if she could heal his scar. This time I got dragged through to a few weeks after my next serious attempt, to talk to a famous alchemist known for healing paranormal beings."

"Was he one of them?" Selene stood and busied herself at the sideboard.

"He was an old vampire who got turned during the Crusades."

"Did you see him?"

"Not this visit. His shop was closed. The jerk in the cape confronted me and told me they'd found the two of you, so that's how I came to rescue you." And got caught in the trap, but they didn't need to know that. "Oh! And the guard was a member of the Order of the Silver Arrow." Now I traced a scratch that, in combination with others, looked like it could have been an arrow at one time.

Selene shuddered. "The ones that don't like us. They took my brother, or tried to. Gabriel defeated their leader."

"Yes, the vargamore Wolfsheim." Could he have been behind the spell change? No, Basil had said someone with similar magic to mine, so it must have been a Fae.

Lonna dug a notepad out of her purse and opened to a blank page. She wrote OSA in a circle in one corner. "Could they have been behind Gabriel and Max's going missing?"

"You two never gave me the details. We were going to discuss that at the ILR."

They exchanged another look, this one questioning. What could they be communicating about?

"There's something we need to tell you." Selene sat beside me. "There was a message for you given to Gabriel before he vanished. The day before, in fact."

"A message? From whom?"

"A male Fae named Ellerin. He called himself the Gray Fae, which Gabriel couldn't find anything about."

"That's because they're not their own category like light and dark Fae. Ellerin does his own thing." And was my father, which I had only discovered recently. "What did he say?"

"That he's gone underground to work on the loose end you couldn't manage."

I frowned, although the message released one of the bands around my heart. Perhaps he hadn't been taken. It might have been the magic hangover from the transitions to and from Faerie and then to and from the past, but I couldn't think of what the rest of the message could mean. "Was there anything else?"

"No. That's all Gabriel said."

Lonna wrote "Ellerin" in another circle in a different corner. "Could he have meant the Order?" She drew a line between them.

"When was the last time you saw Max and Gabriel?" I asked.

Lonna pulled out her phone. "They were going to lunch. Max texted me to let me know they'd be a while. I thought they might have ILR business to discuss, so I didn't question them. Here, it was about ten in the morning." She sighed. "Last Tuesday."

Selene leaned over and rubbed her shoulder. "Make another circle for Reine since she's caught up in this, too."

Lonna did so and drew a line between me and Ellerin. "Does the Order have anything against you?"

I closed my eyes against the memories. "Against me and all

of Faerie. My grandmother wouldn't ally with Wolfsheim, but she kept a close watch on what he did. That's how Rhys and I got caught out—we were spying for her at Culloden. I didn't think Wolfsheim knew we were there, but I can't be certain. Then I helped Gabriel defeat Wolfsheim."

Lonna traced a dotted line between me and the Order. "And your brother?"

"Rhys was helping them for a while in a mercenary role. He's always been more out for himself than the Fae."

"Asshole." Selene bit her lip and turned away. "I'm sorry. I thought I'd forgiven him."

"It's all right. I can't ever decide whether I love him or hate him, and that can change by the moment."

Lonna added Rhys to her diagram and connected him to me and the Order. "Could he have anything to do with Ellerin?"

"They're both part of a committee I put together to rule Faerie in my absence. While I tied up loose ends." The words mocked me. It seemed that whenever I found and tied up one problem, another one unraveled to take its place.

Now all the lines made a web. "It seems," Lonna said, "that we need to figure out who or what is in the middle. Reine, what did you find out in Faerie?"

"That whoever had changed the spell from one of protection to one of entrapment with a time loop has or had powers similar to mine."

"Could it have been Rhys?" Selene asked. "He's your sibling."

"Half-sibling. We have the same mother."

We all looked at each other and then down at the diagram.

"But Maeve—my mother—doesn't have any connection to the Order of the Silver Arrow. Not that I know about, anyway." The very thought squeezed my stomach and made me taste acid.

"And there's no proof," Selene pointed out. "You can't accuse someone without proof."

I didn't tell her that the basis for my exile had been just that. Maeve had accused me of not protecting Rhys, whereas I'd done everything I should have, and he'd run off and gotten himself maimed.

Lonna held the diagram away from her, then tilted it. "I agree there must be some connection to your mother, but wouldn't there have been some trail, especially once you took the throne?"

"Of a secretive Fae working with a hidden society?" I rubbed my burning eyes. "Not necessarily. And I know I defeated her. But Lawrence's mother warned me in a dream, something about Maeve. She wasn't clear, but I thought she meant Maeve tried to corrupt the CPDC..."

"So what now?" Selene asked with a yawn. "I'm exhausted from all that running around."

"Is there anything else you need to tell us, Selene?" Lonna had never been one for subtlety.

"No, I thought there might be, but no..." Selene did something I didn't know she was capable of—she wept. "We've agreed we don't want children, but seeing little Meg..." She sniffled. "Sorry, hormones. I'm PMS-ing and emotional."

"And worried and exhausted and caught in a magical trap we don't know how to get out of," Lonna finished for her. "Come on, let's get you to bed."

She guided Selene into the bedroom, leaving me in the kitchen. Just before she closed the door, Lonna turned and said, "Don't forget what I told you. I'm going to take charge if you don't figure this out. If this is a trap set by a vargamore, then maybe I'm the one for the task."

Her words stung, but she was right. What was I missing? I looked down at her diagram. The only person I could think of who fit in the middle was Maeve. Which meant I needed to talk to Rhys.

But first, if I could dream my way to Faerie, perhaps I could reach Lawrence in his sleep. His mother had warned me, and my mother might be connected to my current predicament, so using my energy to see him warranted a side trip.

17
—————

DOSSIER: PRINCESS REINE

P rague, 15 June, 1809

REPORT BY SIR GERALD BRIGADINE, First Regiment of the Silver Arrow, Tracker Division

DEAR SIR OR MADAM, whoever may be in charge of the Trackers at the moment,

I implore you to convey the urgency of my situation to your superiors, including the Lord Vargamore, Wolfsheim, as I am caught in this blasted time loop and cannot extract myself. I am still only permitted brief forays to watch the Fae, and my desperation led me to an act of which I am heartily ashamed.

The Fae and her cursed brother visited an apothecary shop near the Charles Bridge in Prague, which is from whence I am sending this missive in hopes it reaches you in a speedy fashion. After their

visit, which occurred at sundown, I entered the shop to find it empty, or so I thought.

Whereas I'd had the impression from spying on the Fae during their visit that the apothecary had the feebleness of old age, I found that to be no longer true. He grabbed me from behind, whirled me around, twisted my shirt to cover my silver medallion and throttle my neck, and pinned me to the counter. To my horror, I discovered him to be a vampire. A newly healed lesion on his face betrayed what he had suffered—vampirepox—a typically fatal condition that afflicts the very old, as I understand it. That fact flashed through my mind along with the power this creature must hold now that he'd been restored to himself.

"Hail, and well met," I said, or attempted to. "I am Sir Gerald Brigadine of the Order of the Silver Arrow," and I pointed to the pin on my chest.

He looked at it, then at me, and laughed. "I care not for your Order. In fact, tell Wolfsheim I'll see him in hell for what he's done to me." He let me go, and I crumpled to the floor.

I regained my breath, then asked, "What might that have been?"

"He put me in the attention of the Fae through his rash actions. Do you not think I know the mark of a vargamore blade when I see it? Now I shall have to go into exile."

"But you helped them."

"I gave them something that I told them would take time to try so I could have a window of escape. I now have to leave my home, you piece of excrement."

"If you come to Scotland, I have no doubt that Lord Wolfsheim will protect you."

He only laughed. "I should come to Scotland and kill Wolfsheim myself. It has been a long time since I've tasted the blood of a vargamore."

Because he uttered the forbidden word, which I have recorded not as an insult but of justification, and threatened our leader, I had no choice. I removed the stake from a hidden pouch in my cloak. When he turned his back, I stabbed him. He wheezed a last breath and then dissolved into ash, as his kind does.

I fully admit my guilt in killing a paranormal creature of such age that I have no doubt much wisdom and knowledge have been lost as a result. When I left, I found the nearest church and confessed, although I have not followed the Catholic faith for many years. The priest looked fit to summon the asylum guard, so I slipped out.

I suspect the Fae will return to the apothecary of Bartholemew de Veers once they discover he gave them a sham cure. I recommend you have someone watching the shop so as to trick them into captivity, for this is at least the third life they have disrupted in their quest.

And please, for the love of all the gods, get me out of this time loop!

WITH DESPERATE REGARDS,

Sir Gerald Brigadine

18

LAWRENCE

I turned right out of the neighborhood and headed toward town. The blue sedan followed us through a few side streets, but I got lucky with a light and made a quick turn to merge onto Highway 400. Finally, I lost my pursuer—if that's what they had been—in the evening traffic.

"Did you see what they looked like?" Kestrel asked.

"Only that they had a lot of hair."

"Another Bigfoot?"

"I don't know. The chances of meeting two of those in one day..." I focused on relaxing my grip on the steering wheel so I wouldn't accidentally damage it. "Miniscule at best. The odds of encountering one in a lifetime are pretty impossible."

"'Pretty impossible.' That's imprecise language for you, Uncle."

I smiled, both at her jab and because it was good to hear her teasing again. I hoped these moments of normalcy would occur more often, but I also knew there would still be plenty of grief stabs in between.

When we arrived back at my place, we found the living

room lights blazing. They shone yellow rectangles into the front beds.

"Did you leave the lights on, Kestrel?"

"Nope. Did you."

"No, and they're not on a timer. Stay here."

I didn't pull into the garage. Instead, I let myself in the back door and crept through the mud room and kitchen to the living room, where I found two creatures in gray suits waiting for me. One, another dimension walker, sat in my recliner and peered at a scientific journal through a pair of glasses that looked ridiculously small on his craggy face. The other's paleness betrayed what he was—a vampire—and he seemed to require some effort to lift his gaze from the fireplace to my face.

The urge to change arced through me in a tingling wave, but I shoved it down. I would garg out, as Reine called it, if required, but I preferred to handle things in a civilized way. I couldn't help the extra resonance in my voice when I demanded, "Who the hell are you and what are you doing in my living room?"

"There you are," the Bigfoot said. "Sorry to scare you."

Sir Raleigh, now without the splint, twined between my feet and sat in front of me. He presented a nonthreatening picture at the time, but I knew what he could become.

"Is that a grimalkin?" The vampire scratched the arm of the sofa. "Here, kitty."

Sir Raleigh looked back at me, and I had the sense he would have rolled his eyes if his feline form had been able. He licked his formerly injured leg, which I hoped meant he'd healed.

"I'm going to ask once more, gentle creatures, why are you here?"

Bigfoot closed the journal and stood. The top of his head almost brushed my ceiling fan, and I had twelve-foot ceilings in the living room. "We apologize for frightening you, but we have urgent business."

"Yes," the vamp added and scrambled to his feet. I couldn't tell if he was acting clumsy, or if he had other problems. Or was he hungry?

"What sort of business?"

"Please, have a seat. You and the young lady."

I looked behind me to see that Kestrel had followed me. "I told you to stay in the car."

"Sorry, I came after the cat. I was worried, especially after what you told me." I'd shared with her the injuries my veterinarian colleague had seen.

It was too late for her to turn back, so I took the recliner, and Kestrel the end of the couch nearest it. Our visitors remained standing. Were they trying to intimidate us? The situation had more of an awkwardness to it than anything.

"All right, we've had a seat. Tell us who you are."

The dimension walker folded up his glasses and put them in one of those little tube cases, which he tucked in an inside pocket of his jacket. "I'm Agent Grimm. This is Agent Gilmore. We're with the Normals."

"The what?" They looked anything but.

"We're an agency that helps paranormals to transition to human life. We noticed you talking to one of the high Fae this evening."

Kestrel responded, "Yes, about a potential position on her research team with her adviser at UGA."

"Is that all?"

"That's all the useful information we got," I grumbled. "And it's none of your business."

The vampire spoke. "That's not entirely true. You see, when someone goes through our program to settle into a non-paranormal, that is to say, normal, existence, they renounce contact with and discussion of paranormal affairs. I believe Lilith spoke with you of another Fae princess."

"'Another?'" Kestrel shot me a shocked look. "She's a princess like Reine?"

Grimm glared at Gilmore. "She is a graduate student at the University of Georgia, nothing more."

That was interesting. I'd have to ask Reine if she knew this Lilith, or "Lily," as she called herself. If I could ever talk to Reine again.

"So you're here to warn us away from her?" I asked. "I assure you, gentlemen, we were not trying to convert her back to paranormal life."

"No," Grimm growled, "but merely being around you, especially considering the long history of gargoyles and Fae, could tempt her back to the life she left."

"Is she a nun?" Kestrel asked. I nudged her foot with mine.

Gilmore smirked, but Grimm didn't look amused when he replied, "No, we do not mandate worship of human gods or dictate the bounds of sexual activities."

Kestrel turned pink, and I had to try not to laugh at the ridiculousness of it all. Then it struck me. "Is Grand-Pied one of you as well?"

Grimm turned his scowl to me. "He is in a trial phase. Consequently, we need for you to stay away from him as well."

I stood. "Well, thank you for this visit, gentlemen. This was most enlightening. But considering that you belong to a rogue organization with no power to enforce anything, I can't say I'm going to take your warning too seriously."

"Big words from a gargoyle whose house we entered. It's warded, is it not?"

"Yes, but not against dimension walkers and vampires. I can rectify that." I hoped. Another thing to ask Reine.

"And we are but two of many different creatures in the Normals. You can't possibly ward against us all."

Kestrel and I exchanged worried glances. We were in this way over our heads, and we didn't have anyone to go to. I wouldn't know how to access the Truth Seekers, and they only got involved with paranormal creatures interfering with humans. At least that was my understanding.

"Is that a threat, Agent Grimm?"

"Only if you wish it to be, Doctor Gordon."

"What's with all the G names?" Kestrel muttered.

Gilmore pulled a business card case from a pocket inside his jacket and extracted a card with his long, tapered fingers. He handed it to Kestrel. "Please get in touch if you ever want more information."

I wanted to pluck the card from her hand, but I managed to squash the impulse. I had to remind myself I wasn't her parent, and she had too much sense to fall for their false promises. There was no way someone like us could be completely "normal," whatever that meant.

"Remember what we told you," Grimm said with a final frown. "Stay away from Lilith and Grand-Pied." He put a hand on Gilmore's shoulder, and they both vanished. Air rushed to fill the space with a pop, and an otherworldly chill eddied through the room.

I held my hand out for the card. "I can get rid of that for you."

"No, it's fine. I'll keep it." She stuck it in her pocket.

"You can't seriously be thinking of accepting their invitation. You know there's no such thing as 'normal.'"

She shrugged. "I'm not at the moment, but who knows? I've definitely had enough of the paranormal world. What is there for me in it anymore, anyway?"

"There's me. You heard them—you'd have to renounce all your connections."

"But they can't mean family."

"I don't know. They sounded pretty strict." My heart did a panicked tarantella in my throat. She couldn't be seriously considering... I didn't know what. "You've heard that no one should make major decisions while they're grieving. There is some wisdom in that advice."

"Yeah." She cast her gaze to the ground, where Sir Raleigh looked up at her with sadness in his green eyes. She crouched down to scratch him behind the ears. "But you're going to join Reine in Faerie and leave me, so I have to think about what I'm going to do. I don't have to make any decisions tonight."

"Or not until after you finish school. I won't leave you alone —you know that."

She straightened, and she swiped at her eyes. "That's what I thought about my parents, too." She clenched her fist. "And if I'm in an organization like the Normals, I won't be tempted to use my powers, especially not the necromancy one."

In that moment, I saw two potential paths for her. One led to a quiet human life, which she would probably find boring, and the other the way of the Trickster, which would lead to more pain and chaos. And I had no control over which one she chose.

"You're smart. You may be tempted, but you won't give in."

"Again, you're forgetting who my parents were. Both of them gave into an impulse and look where it got them. I have to protect myself, Uncle Lawrence. I have to protect the world."

"That's a lot for someone who barely has two decades under her belt. Go on to bed. You're exhausted. We can talk about this later."

"You're right." She walked over and kissed me on the cheek, then turned. "Come on, Raleigh. It's bedtime. Will you come purr me to sleep?"

The cat-shaped grimalkin trotted after her. She went down the hallway toward the guest rooms, but Sir Raleigh turned back toward me and gave me a look that said, *This is far from over.*

Unfortunately, I had to agree with him.

19

REINE

My dream brought me to a bench by a small lake. Trees lined the shoreline, some of which I couldn't see since the edge of the water formed little coves. That disturbed me—too many places for the wrong kind of surprise to pop out. I didn't know if my strategy had worked, if I'd managed to invoke some part of the Collective Unconscious to meet Lawrence in. This place didn't look familiar, but I had that "oh, I know where this is" dream feeling. I needed to go with the dream's flow, and it would carry me where I needed.

I also reminded myself that, no matter what happened, I had to pay attention to details since they would hold the clues in this strange otherworld of symbolism and imagery.

Starting with the bench... The wood and wrought iron of the bench invoked an old public park aesthetic, and I sat on it and gazed over the water. I placed my hands on my lap and found I wore a blue flowered sundress and silver strapped sandals with chunky imitation wicker heels. All right, then, I was dressed for a date. Hopefully someone I wanted to see would come along.

That someone appeared momentarily. Lawrence walked out of a gap in the trees to my right, and I "remembered" that's where the parking area must have been. He wore khaki pants, a white linen button-down shirt open at the collar and rolled up to the elbows, and he carried a picnic basket, out of which stuck a baguette and the stem of a wine bottle.

Definitely old school date script.

"Reine!" He set the basket down and closed the distance between us in three long strides. I jumped into his arms, and he held me against him. "Where have you been? I've been worried sick about you."

The question then became—was this truly him, or dream Lawrence doing what I expected of him? How could I find out?

I couldn't, and that turned into a frustration that piled on the others, a Jenga tower in my chest that could fall and clatter into a nervous breakdown at any moment. I would have to play along.

"I'm stuck in a time loop that's centered on a witch's cottage in the Scottish Highlands."

My words didn't seem to dent his awareness. Damn. "What is this place?" He went to retrieve the picnic basket.

"I don't know. I was hoping you'd tell me."

He looked around, and his customary frown line appeared between his brows. "It reminds me of a park I used to go to when I was in veterinary school. I haven't thought about it in years."

"Did you bring girls there?"

He grinned. "No, I wasn't much for dating. Too obsessed about, you know…"

I spoke around the lump of sorrow in my throat. "Finding who killed your father."

"Yes. I used to come here and think. Played through those memories over and over when studying got to be too much."

"Only you would think of puzzling through your greatest trauma as a viable break activity."

He shrugged, then looked at his wrist. "How much time do we have here?"

That was one clue. Instead of continuing our banter, he'd gotten back down to business. But again, was that what I expected or truly him?

"I don't know. It's hard to accurately infer the passage of time in this place."

"The park?"

"The Collective Unconscious. Go ahead and unpack the picnic?"

He spread out the red checkered cloth, on which he placed more food and utensils than could have possibly fit in the basket had it been subject to normal laws of physics. The wine and glasses stood up without efforts to seek a flat enough spot for them, and everything looked fresh, including the Greek salad, which would have started to wilt as soon as the vinaigrette hit the leaves. The baguette maintained its form, and he also brought out different spreads including my favorite, roasted eggplant.

He uncorked the wine—or, more accurately, when he picked it up, the cork disappeared—and he poured two glasses of the clear golden liquid. Then he handed one to me.

"Here's to the Collective Unconscious, then. I keep forgetting this isn't a dream."

"I don't, but I'm enjoying it." I sipped the wine, which tasted as I would have expected, like a dry Riesling with notes of honey.

"But we need to talk, to figure out how to get you out of... What did you say? A time loop?" He rubbed his eyes. "I need to stay focused. But it's so hard."

"Yes, a time loop or bubble. Same thing. Someone took the

protection spell I cast over the cottage and twisted it—at least that's what Basil told me when I went to see him in Faerie."

"You went to Faerie to talk to Troubadour before coming to see me?" He looked down to spoon some sort of cheese dip over a slice of bread, and I couldn't read the expression in his eyes.

"I had to, so I could see if there was an easy solution to the loop. I also had a warning from your mother before that."

"In a dream?"

"Yes, she somehow managed to reach out to me. She warned me that a powerful enemy is in motion, and, oh! She also asked what a Cimex is. I thought he was in jail."

"They let him out considering he wasn't acting of his own volition, even though his emotions drove him." He sliced a piece of bread and handed it to me. "And he wasted no time in cutting me off from the CPDC and putting me on a 'mandatory bereavement leave' so I could attend to Kestrel."

"How is she?" A guilt mole wriggled in my chest every time I thought about how I'd kept Kestrel from saving her adoptive father, even though the consequences would have been so much worse.

"She's hanging in there." His expression softened slightly. "She kidded and laughed today. It was good to see." Then he closed his eyes, and that line appeared again. "Have you ever heard of an organization called the Normals?"

"No. What's that?"

"They help supernatural creatures to 'assimilate' into human society." He snorted. "It's circular, isn't it? Considering the variation in human society and how there's no true normal. They tried to recruit her, and she seemed open to it."

Something in the air shifted, and a chill gust of air ruffled my hair. The cheese and cracker, which had formerly been bread, disappeared. Dark clouds gathered over the lake, and the wind picked up.

Sir Raleigh appeared, and he ran toward me, meowing. I gathered him up, and I could at least tell he was his real self.

"What is it?" Lawrence stood. "We should get to shelter." He shook his head. "I mean, can you change it?"

"I think the date script is encouraging us to have a wet clothing contest, and then huddle together under the picnic blanket in the small shelter over there." Indeed, a covered picnic area had appeared among the trees to the left.

Large drops pelted down, and the food and wine disappeared. Lawrence gathered up the picnic blanket, and we ran for the shelter. By the time we got there, we had both been soaked through, but we laughed.

What had we been talking about? The memory of the conversation fled like wisps of fog, especially after Lawrence wrapped me in the picnic blanket and then plucked a piece of grass from my hair. He smiled at me, and I tilted my head back to receive his kiss.

That confirmed it was him, especially as the kisses grew more urgent, and I perched on one of the tables. He ran his hand up my leg and under my dress, and his other hand found my waist and then the zipper at the back of the sundress, which he unzipped. I slid my hands up his hard abs and pecs, and his shirt disappeared.

A sharp pain in my left ankle made me break the kiss with an "ow!" Sir Raleigh had reached up and caught the back of my shin in his mouth, not biting hard enough to break skin, but it got my attention.

"This is a dream. I mean, it needs to not be a dream." I pushed Lawrence away, and Raleigh let go.

Lawrence blinked a couple of times, and then nodded. "Yes, we need to figure out how to get you out of that time loop and who's driving all of this. Did Basil give you any idea who may have altered your spell?"

"Only someone with similar magic to mine, which means

any light Fae."

"What about your mother?"

Irritation flared through my gut at the suggestion, and I snapped, "I don't know. And even if it was her, I wouldn't have any idea how to go about finding her."

"Hey," he said and lifted my chin so my gaze met his. "I know it's hard to think about, but you have to acknowledge the possibility. And it fits her style, working behind the scenes."

"I know, but that makes the problem harder to solve. Oh, and the Order of the Silver Arrow is somehow involved, too."

"The vargamore's organization?"

"That's them." I related the journey into Prague and how I'd almost been trapped. "But then the trip ended. No matter where I go, I end up back at the cottage."

"I wish you would end up with me."

"Me, too."

He hugged me to him, and I relished the rain-soaked stone scent of his skin. The rain itself pitted the surface of the lake and made a romantic clatter on the metal roof. Before I knew it, we were kissing again, and I didn't object when my dress disappeared. His hands cupped my breasts, and I wrapped my legs around his butt. Without our kiss breaking, the scene shifted to the two of us being naked and wrapped in the picnic cloth on the table. He kissed down my neck and took one of my nipples in his mouth, and electric shocks of pleasure mixed with need coursed through me. Our lovemaking proceeded with dream speed, and soon we both climaxed.

When we finished, a gray tail swiped over my face, and I glanced up to see Sir Raleigh looking down with feline disapproval.

A roaring sensation overtook the rain, and although Lawrence held me, the dream faded. Before it did, he asked, "Would a dimension-walker be able to help?"

"It's worth a try!" I shouted into the darkness.

20

————

LAWRENCE

The first thing I did after I woke up from the dream of —visit from?—Reine was take a cold shower. A long cold shower. It cooled my libido, which wanted to have her physically in my bed and not only in the dream world. It didn't do much for the ache in my chest that our separation continued to pull at, especially now that I knew why she hadn't contacted me. A time loop, of all the weird things. That reeked of Fae magic, as she'd told me, and I questioned her blind spot around her mother's potential involvement. But when would Maeve have had the opportunity to change the spell without Reine knowing?

While Reine was on the run with Rhys. Or at any time after when she'd wandered far enough from the area to not sense her mother's meddling. But why hadn't it caught her when she'd gone back?

Or had she? She'd tended to avoid things that reminded her of Rhys' maiming and their resulting exile, to the point of hating gargoyles. Her mother would have known that.

No one played the long game like the Fae. That thought, more than the shower, chilled me to my marrow.

I emerged to find my phone blinking with a text from Latonya Francis. *"Have update for you. Meet me at the cafe off Ashford-Dunwoody."* She named a familiar place, where I'd sometimes met up with John and Beverly before we all headed into work. Now sadness wrapped the missing Reine ache, and I had to catch my breath before I responded that I'd see her there in twenty minutes.

Kestrel seemed to still be asleep, and I didn't see any sign of Sir Raleigh, so I supposed he'd gone back to Kestrel after finding us in the CU. I didn't want to open the door to her room to check for fear of waking her from whatever comfort sleep brought to her grief, so I left her a note letting her know I'd gone to meet a colleague for breakfast.

The morning rush made for a crowd, but I spotted Latonya's dark face and close-cropped hair when she waved from a table in the corner. I wove through the closely packed tables and attempted to not trip over the briefcases, laptop bags, and school bags that took up more real estate on the floor than they needed to. Or perhaps fatigue made me clumsy.

"You look like Hades," she told me. "Here, I got you a skim latte. Figured it would be easier than waiting for the server to come back."

"Thanks." I sipped the foamy drink. "It's just what I needed."

"Seriously, are you sleeping?" She glanced over my shoulder, then back to me.

I checked the view behind me in the glass of a photo frame and couldn't see anyone or anything suspicious. "Sort of. Doctor River is missing." I used the name Reine gave herself for when she dealt with humans—Doctor Renee River.

"I'm sorry to hear that. I'm afraid the news I have for you isn't going to help you feel better."

"Did you find out anything about Cimex?"

She looked around again, then leaned closer and lowered

her voice so I had to strain to hear her over the crowd din. "Only that he's started the process to get you fired."

"What? He told me to take a leave of absence."

"He's doing it on grounds that you're withholding crucial information from an investigation into someplace called...The Aerie?" She wrinkled her nose. "I've never heard of it."

"No, most people haven't. And by people, I mean non-gargoyles. It's a well-kept secret among my kind."

"Oh." Her eyes and mouth made the same round shape. "Is that where they all are now?"

"I don't know the answer to that. Only that it's secret for a reason."

"That reason being the Fae? The gargoyles needed some-where to be safe."

"Something like that." I couldn't tell her everything, and I decided to exclude that I'd recently been to The Aerie. "What's with his sudden obsession? And do you know anything about why they brought him back?"

She sighed and dropped her gaze to her half-full latte cup. "Only that someone powerful wanted him there. I don't know, Lawrence. Things have been weird since Beverly died. Even before, if I'm honest about it."

"Do your other contacts know anything?" I dared not say Robert Cannon's name out loud, but she would ferret out infor-mation for him occasionally. That was one reason I'd asked her to help me.

She shook her head. "They haven't been in touch."

"Someone powerful, and an obsession with a place designed to protect gargoyles from the Fae." I put down the latte. I didn't need the caffeine to make my tension headache worse. What would my dentist think about my recent uptick in teeth grinding? Again, all signs pointed to Maeve. But that wasn't why I'd asked for Latonya's help. Well, not the main reason. "Did you learn anything about professor Grand-Pied?"

She pulled a file from her bag. "This was all I could find. Don't open it here. You'll see there's not much to go on, but you know we're not supposed to bring this stuff out."

"I'm aware. Thank you." I slipped the folder into my own leather satchel. "Can you give me an overview?"

"He only came to the attention of the CPDC a few years ago. That a dimension-walker drew the notice of our watchers is strange enough, but that's not the oddest thing. You'll see there's a strange notation on the corner of each page. NRML. Do you know what it means?"

"I can guess." Somehow one of our colleagues in the Registry knew of the existence of my unwelcome visitors. "Have you heard of an organization called The Normals?"

"No." She picked up her cup and drained it but didn't meet my eyes. Liar.

"Are you sure?"

"We hear rumors of strange and secret organizations in our line of work all the time, Lawrence. It's possible someone mentioned them, and I didn't pay attention." The table shifted slightly as she uncrossed her legs and recrossed them the other way. I couldn't read other paranormals' auras like Reine sometimes could, but I didn't need to. The question had made Latonya uncomfortable.

"Well, I may or may not have met a couple of them last night. They're after Kestrel to join them so she can ditch all the painful supernatural stuff and live as a human. Which would mean she'd have to renounce all her paranormal connections. That's why I'm taking an interest."

"And those connections would include you?"

I nodded since I couldn't even get the word "yes" out through a throat too constricted with the potential grief of losing Kestrel's parents—my best friends—and possibly their daughter, too.

"What does she want?"

"She's too young to make that kind of decision, especially in the throes of her grief. You know that sorrow makes people unable to think straight."

"Oh, I'm well aware." She gazed off past my shoulder again, but I could tell she'd turned her attention inward rather than to something behind me. "I can't say that helps clarify anything for me, but I would say to be careful. If there's an organization that wants to help paranormals hide and has been successful in doing so, I would question their means and their motive."

"Thank you. I'm glad you're also suspicious of them."

"I'm opposed to any organization that keeps me from getting my data, and those who join them are lost to us." She glanced at her watch. "I have to go so Lucius doesn't get suspicious. I won't tell him hi for you."

"Bastard," I growled.

She dropped a twenty on the table. "Here, this should cover my drink and the chocolate croissant I had while I was waiting for you. Will you be okay?"

"Without Kestrel or without my job or without Reine?" The multiple potential losses dizzied me like I teetered on the edge of an abyss of despair.

"All of the above."

I hated that she made me give an honest answer, but that was one of the reasons I'd both feared and respected her. "I'll be fine without my job. Paranormals as old as I am have other means of support. As for the other two..." I shook my head since that damn thread had tied my airway shut again.

She patted me on the shoulder, and I had to not flinch away from the awkwardness. "Be careful. The one thing you can't live without is your life."

With that, she left me with more questions. What had she not been telling me?

I ordered another latte and two croissants, one chocolate and one ham and cheese, all to go. I didn't feel like going back to my house, so I took the food and the drink to a nearby park. After checking to make sure I was alone, I opened the file she'd given me. As she'd said, most of the information hadn't been filled in like area of origin or age, but that strange combination of letters had been stamped on the corner of all the pages. Had someone known? Or had the Normals infiltrated us? It didn't make sense that they'd advertise their presence, so that means someone in our system had identified Grand-Pied as one of them. The other dimension-walker Agent Grimm—like he was the one with the top-secret government job, not me—had said that Grand-Pied was in a trial period. And they'd warned me away from Lilith.

That brought me to a new question... Were the Normals an organization that helped paranormals who didn't want to deal with the magical world anymore or a cult? And if so, to what lengths would they go to get their paws on Kestrel?

I didn't have time to ponder that question because my phone rang. I looked down to see my mother was calling.

Since she'd asked Reine about Cimex, I eagerly answered, but no one was there.

Another warning? Or a threat? A cloud moved over the sun and cast the day—and my brain—into sudden chill, and I scrambled to gather my things before the first raindrops soaked the papers into illegibility.

Why hadn't I checked more closely on Kestrel before I left?

21

REINE

I paced the floorboards in front of the hearth until Selene and Lonna woke. By that time, I'd discovered the cottage to be approximately ten paces across without furniture, which would add another couple. Useless information, but something to keep part of my mind active while I thought through everything Lawrence had told me. Including that he'd met a dimension-walker, presumably in an urban area. What could be happening to bring them out of the woods and wilderness and into the cities? The thought chilled me and added to the growing list of puzzles and problems.

The two lycanthropes emerged from the bedroom and blinked at the sunlight streaming through the windows. Sparkling flecks of dust whirled to their own silent music. That gave me a thought... What sort of music was I expecting to hear, and what should I be listening for?

"How did you sleep?" I asked.

Lonna pulled a pick from her purse and ran it through her curly hair, and Selene rubbed her eyes. "Strangely," Selene said. "Odd dreams and feelings, fragments more than anything, danced through my brain all night."

She'd used a word I had just thought, and I tried to keep the heat from blooming in my chest, neck, and face, but it didn't work. I'm sure I turned bright pink. "What sort of fragments?"

Her own face turned pink, and if I could have died of embarrassment—but not shame, because I had no regrets from my nocturnal rom-com dream visit to Lawrence—I would have. She waved the question away with, "Oh, I don't know. I can't remember any details."

I opted not to call her on the lie.

"So what's the plan?" Lonna looked at her phone and sighed. "I keep hoping something will come through. How much time is passing in our timeline while we're stuck here? Will I come out to find Abby's grown into an adult doomed to be bitter since both her parents disappeared?" She twisted her hair into a messy bun at the top of her head. "And why haven't I needed to wash my hair yet?"

"I don't know," I admitted. "How are you two holding up? Are you hungry?"

They exchanged glances. "We weren't going to say anything," Selene admitted, "but yes, although not as much as I would have expected."

"I may have seen some berries outside." Not a lie, but I didn't remember if I'd noticed them before or after we crossed the boundary into the time loop. "I can see if they're still there. Hang tight."

I crossed the threshold and closed the door behind me, but Lonna's voice floated out to me, "I wish she would find us some nice steaming cups of coffee as well."

I didn't want to reveal too much of my Fae magic, but I did briefly consider bringing them some coffee or tea I'd "found." Perhaps I could conjure up some tea leaves.

A movement in my peripheral vision caught my attention, and I looked over to see a new plant had sprung up. It didn't look familiar, but the serrated leaves had a smell that tickled my memory. Tea? But that didn't grow here.

What was I thinking? I couldn't expect things to make sense. I whispered a prayer of thanks to whichever god had gifted us the plant and picked enough leaves to make three cups. I dried and aged them with a simple spell. Then I put them in the pouch that had appeared at my belt because why not?

My mind whirred, and I continued my search for food. I considered forming an intention for a mythical Southeastern US macaroni and cheese plant, since the dish always ended up on "vegetable" plates, but decided that would be carrying things too far. I couldn't lie due to my Fae nature, and I needed to see how far this wishing would go.

And why wouldn't it allow me to wish my way out of the predicament?

A gentle breeze lifted my hair off my shoulder, and when I went to catch it, I found a familiar purring presence that nearly made me topple with his sudden weight.

"Sir Raleigh!" He crawled into my arms and didn't object right away when I hugged him tightly to me. Indeed, he purred. "I'm so glad you're here."

"It let me through." His words always surprised me when they came into my mind with the clarity of Ellerin's voice. I hoped that meant the time loop would let him leave as well since he was a creature of the Fae.

"I'm so glad it did." I placed him on the ground, and he sniffed around.

With tail held high, he walked straight to a bush heavy with blackberries, and strawberry plants peeked out from underneath. A basket appeared beside them, and I picked enough for two people and a Fae to have for breakfast.

When I entered the cottage, Selene and Lonna stood behind one of the chairs, and Lonna pointed a broom handle at the kettle that had been hanging beside the hearth and now sat within it. It swung and steamed.

"What happened?" I asked.

"It disappeared and reappeared there."

"Good," I said and grabbed a cloth with which to hold the metal handle, which no doubt would burn me otherwise. "It's time for breakfast and tea."

Lonna looked from me to the kettle, and then back at me. "Where did you get all that?"

"In the garden."

"Even the pouch and the basket?"

"Yes. Did you happen to look in the bread box to see if there's a loaf?"

"Yes," Selene replied with a sigh. "But there wasn't."

"Look again."

Indeed, bread had appeared. I didn't know what, but something had shifted. I only hoped it wasn't the protective spell kicking in because the time loop spell had decided we were to be permanent guests, so it might as well accommodate us.

"What does this mean?" Lonna held Selene back to keep her from grabbing the loaf. "If we eat it, will we be stuck here forever?"

"This is a time loop, not Hades, although I can see the similarity. Let me think for a second."

Sir Raleigh appeared and twined around my ankles, and Lonna and Selene both scrambled back.

"Is he real?"

I reached down to scratch his soft ears. "Yes, he said the time loop let him through. Raleigh, can we eat the things that have appeared?"

He nodded, and he didn't say directly, but he confirmed my suspicion.

"He says yes, and that the protection spell I originally wove over the cabin is providing for us."

Selene wasted no time bringing the bread out and slicing off thick hunks. "Is that what you intended it to do?"

"Not exactly. It was more of a spell that only those with good intentions would be able to find Irina, but something strange happened the night of the Battle of Culloden. Plus, it's quite likely the spell has degraded through the centuries, which means it's trying to adapt so it doesn't die."

So what did that mean about the time loop?

I made the tea, and we sat to eat while it steeped. The berries and bread made for a decent breakfast, especially since the bread had a sweet flavor like challah or brioche. It would have made a nice French toast. Would the spell give us eggs, too, if we asked? Or chickens we'd need to take care of? I'd hate to abandon them once we left.

If we left.

Once we'd eaten, cleared the dishes, and sat blowing over the rims of our mugs to cool them, Lonna asked, "What now? No, I'm tired of sitting here while you go do all the interesting things. Selene and I must have something we can do to help get us un-stuck. Test for weak spots in the spell's bubble, something like that."

I gave her one of those chin-down, eyebrows-up looks over the top of my mug. "Because going through the weak spot last time worked out oh-so-very well."

Selene jumped in, as I'd noticed she liked to do. What did the constant tension between me and Lonna feel like for the empathetic werewolf? And did she feel the fear of her prey when she hunted? Did it help or hinder her? I'd have to ask once we got out of this mess.

"The weak spot happened because Reine got dragged through. We saw her. Maybe if we can catch that guy... Who is he, Reine?"

"I don't know. But he's been popping in and out watching

us. Watching me, rather. I don't know that he cares about the two of you."

Lonna spread her hands. "Then it sounds like you need to have a conversation with him. Maybe he can help us."

"You don't think that's what I was trying to do when he ran away? That's why I lassoed him."

She rubbed her neck, and the guilt mole stirred in the recesses of my guts.

"Maybe you startled him?" Selene asked.

"Perhaps... I did wake to find him standing over me."

"Doing what?" Lonna put her cup down. "Was he going to harm you?"

"I... I don't know." My least favorite phrase. "I only saw his feet. Did you two notice anything?"

Selene shook her head. "Only when you cried out, but by the time we got to the window, you were already being dragged through. He's fast."

But why had he been standing there, so close? If I'd come upon someone sleeping and wanted them to wake, I'd nudge them, or if I was going to wait, I'd stand back so they wouldn't harm me.

An image flashed through my mind of him raising a sword to plunge it through me, and I shuddered. "I think he was trying to kill me. But I don't know why."

"And that gives us all the more reason to work harder on getting out of here. What if he kills you and comes after us next?"

"Thanks, Lonna. It's not like I'm not trying."

Selene laid a hand on Lonna's arm. "What else did you find out in your dreaming?"

I thought back through it and realized I'd done most of the talking. Damn. But Lawrence had told me a few things... I related what he'd said about Cimex cutting him off from the

CPDC, the Normals approaching Kestrel, and his having encountered a dimension-walker.

Selene wrinkled her nose. "A what? Something about the name disturbs me. A lot."

"You probably know them as Bigfoot creatures. That's how they tend to appear to humans, anyway. And you should be disturbed. No one really knows what they are or their intentions."

Lonna interrupted my lesson with, "And now for the useful question... Can they help us?"

"Yes, if Lawrence can approach him and get him to agree. We're essentially caught in a dimension, a time bubble, between the waking world and Faerie, and possibly touching the Collective Unconscious as well. It's hard for us to move between just two, if you think about it, and that's usually what people are limited to. Fae, too. We can go between your world and ours, but it takes extra effort to go into the CU. The dimension-walkers can move between all of them, and they appear differently in each one."

"So how do they appear in Faerie?" Selene asked.

"I don't know. I've never seen one or heard of one going there. Maybe they're like gargoyles—they can't breathe our air. Or something like that."

Lonna was making notes again. "So could one come here?"

"Yes, since this loop, this bubble, was rooted in a place in your world, the atmosphere is the same. That's why we can all breathe it."

"What do we do to make it easier for him, assuming he cooperates? You said 'he,' right? Do they have females?"

"I don't know what the dimension-walker genders are. That's how mysterious they've been, and resistant to study. It's rude to ask too many questions about an unfamiliar species." I glared at her, hoping she'd get the hint.

"Noted. But my other question remains."

"I don't know that, either." I was saying that a lot this morning. Afternoon? Whatever the time happened to be. It definitely moved differently here. "It seems we should still focus on what we can do rather than waiting for a male of whatever persuasion to rescue us."

Selene snickered, and Lonna rolled her eyes. "So, we'll test for weak spots. You keep working on dreaming. What have you learned so far?"

"That my efforts to find a cure for Rhys' maimed face were unsuccessful, but I knew that. There has to be something more, something to the strange symbols I've seen at the end of the visitations."

"What symbols?" Selene asked. "I wish I could get to the internet so I could look them up." She cast her gaze upward. "Oh, most powerful spell, could you install Wi-Fi?"

No answer, and I couldn't help a giggle. "Nice try, but the spell can only provide what it knows. And the symbols were like sideways Ys, but they're different. The first had two long branches, but the last one only had one short and one long. Like the lopsided horns of a snail. I'll continue to ponder them."

"We will, too." Lonna sighed, and a wistful expression flitted across her features. "I wish Max was here. He'd know, or he'd know how to find out."

"I know." I couldn't say anything except to make another internal prayer that Lawrence would stay safe. And help us. "All right, I'm going to dream again. See if I can figure out the key to getting us out of here."

22

LAWRENCE

I rushed home to find Kestrel engaged in an epic battle... with a box of cereal.

"I can never get these stupid bags open," she grumbled, then added, "Hey, Uncle Lawrence. Where've you been?"

I held up the bag with the chocolate croissant I'd picked up for her. "Met a colleague for breakfast. I'm trying to figure out what's going on at the CPDC, and I was hoping they could give me some more info on Grand-Pied."

"Yeah, about that..." The bag finally tore, and sugary flakes of doom scattered all over the kitchen, or that's how it seemed. "Whoops. Is the thing in the paper bag for me?"

"Yes, but first I'll help you clean up. I'm surprised Sir Raleigh isn't in here with you."

Kestrel fetched the broom from the pantry. "He left sometime last night. I haven't seen him. Isn't he with you?"

"No." I hoped he'd gone to fetch help for Reine, that I wouldn't have to have this conversation. I'd been over it several times in my head while I drove, and each time it ended badly. I hoped it would go differently, but I knew Kestrel. She had her mother's stubborn streak and her father's ability to hold a grudge.

"Did you see him last night?"

"In a sense. I took a trip to the Collective Unconscious." There, reel her in with an interesting tidbit.

Indeed, she paused in her sweeping and looked up. "How do you know it wasn't a dream?"

"It was a dream, too. It even had a script it kept trying to push on us."

She wrinkled her nose. "Us?"

"Yes, Reine called me there."

"Oh." She dropped her gaze and focused on the scattered cereal like it held the key to deciphering the mysteries of the universe.

"She's in trouble, Kestrel. She's caught in a time loop."

"Sucks to be her." Yes, that was how I'd foreseen her reaction. Then, she asked, "So what does that mean? Is it like a *Groundhog Day* scenario?"

"Something like that. I don't fully understand them. There's supposedly a syndrome that can happen to people when they're stuck in them for too long, like they lose their sense of time in the real world, which can make them insane."

"I would guess Fae are used to slippery time stuff, Uncle. She'll be fine."

"Except for the part where she's stuck."

She shrugged, then disappeared behind the island when she bent to sweep the human kibble into the dustpan. She straightened and said, "Well, what does she expect you to do about it? She's supposed to be the queen, right? She should be able to figure it out."

"Except she's stuck, and it won't let her out. I need to bring in help on this one, and I'm stuck with no allies."

"What about my f—Ellerin?"

"He's vanished, too."

She stopped. "Did she kill him as well?"

"She didn't kill your father." I hoped I hadn't snapped at her, but she ducked her head and turned away to dump the cereal in the trash. I walked over to her and discarded the handful I'd picked up, then rubbed her shoulder. "She kept you from doing something stupid, something that would have affected your entire future in a bad way."

She jerked away. "She should have let me make that choice. I could have saved him."

"And turned him into what? A zombie? Or something worse?"

"At least he would still be alive. Still be here to talk to me about stuff, like school, and..." She turned back to me. "When you said help, you didn't mean Professor Grand-Pied, did you?"

"He's a dimension walker. She said he could help." At least that's what I thought she'd shouted after me, and I would take any direction I could get.

"But he's already mad at us. And so are the Normals."

"I'm glad to hear you're not thrilled about them anymore."

"No. I don't want their help, don't need their help, to be a normal college kid. I can take care of that myself, but only if you give me the chance."

"What do you mean, give you the chance?"

"If you go to Grand-Pied, you draw him into this whole thing—this Reine drama that keeps sucking you back when..."

"When what?"

"Nothing. But it's bad enough she's ruined my life by not saving Mom and not letting me save Dad. I don't want saving her, or trying to, to piss off Professor Grand-Pied even more. If he does help you, he'll feel like you owe him a favor, and what if that turns into me owing him a favor, and he doesn't want to bring me on as a research assistant?"

I blinked, trying to follow her logic. "So you're saying that by asking for his help, I'm going to bias him against you? This has nothing to do with you, with your college career."

"You think so? You don't see how everything is connected, how convoluted it can get? Look at what happened last night. We met with Lily. Then those creeps followed us home and ambushed us."

"So it was okay to talk to her about asking him to help with the Faerie atmosphere situation, but not extracting Reine from a time loop?"

She dumped another dustpan full of sugar flakes into the trash. "The atmosphere thing is a scientific quandary. The time loop is a personal favor, and we don't need this getting personal."

"How can you say it's not already personal? She's my mate, Kestrel. She and I are bonded, and she is in trouble, and it is my job to take care of her." The urge to change into my gargoyle form exploded from the base of my brain and down my nerves in an electric torrent. I clenched my fists to try to stop it, and my emerging claws dug into my palms. I managed to keep the transformation in check, but with every ounce of willpower. When I spoke, it was in my deep, resonant gargoyle voice. "As it has been since before this planet birthed the scourge that is humanity."

She dropped the broom and dustpan, then turned to me, wide-eyed. "Is that how you think of me, as a scourge?"

Guilt washed in an icy flood down my veins and chilled the urge to garg out.

"No, although you're not human. And I don't think of humanity as a scourge, either. I don't know where that came from." Or I didn't want to know. Could some ancient part of my own brain hold the key to the puzzle that was the gargoyles' exile from Faerie?

"I am so human. I'm done with being a paranormal. So what if I have lots of different powers? They're nearly impossible to use, and I don't have anyone to train me. Not anyone who I want to, anyway," she added before I could suggest that Reine might be willing.

"Then if you're not going to help me, step aside and allow me to do what I need to do."

"Fine. Go ahead and talk to the Bigfoot. But know that if you do, and if you screw things up for me, I'm done with you. If you're not going to take care of me, then step aside and let *me* do what I need to do."

Coming from her, my words sounded harsher than I'd meant them to. My heart cracked wide like the rift that had opened between us.

"I won't screw things up for you, but this is a matter of life and death, Kestrel."

"Things have gotten screwed up ever since that Fae came to Atlanta, and there's already been plenty of death. Why should now be any different?" She grabbed the bag with the croissant in it and walked out. I looked around for Sir Raleigh to give me a similar angry look, but remembered that he'd gone, too.

"What am I going to do?" I asked the empty kitchen. When I stepped forward to grab my phone, a flake crunched under my shoe. With a sigh, I grabbed the broom and dustpan and finished cleaning up the kitchen. Unfortunately, my relationship with Kestrel wouldn't be tidied so easily.

Even so, I'd already thought through how I could get back to Athens and do what human researchers and cryptid hunters had failed at for decades—corner the elusive Bigfoot.

23

LAWRENCE

Several hours later, I stood outside of the social sciences building where I knew Doctor Grand-Pied would be holding office hours for his summer classes. I hoped he hadn't decided to do them remotely, but I also recalled something about dimension-walkers screwing with electrical equipment, so perhaps he'd meet with students the old-fashioned way. Although I'd wished I could stay close to my mother while I did my training, I don't think I would have opted to do anything remote. There was something about face-to-face learning that couldn't be replicated through a screen.

Indeed, Grand-Pied emerged from the side entrance to the building a few minutes later. I intended to walk with him to his car, but his long strides took him up Jackson Street toward downtown Athens itself. Intrigued, I followed. Plus, I couldn't catch up to him without running, and I didn't want to draw undue attention to myself.

He crossed Broad, and I barely made it before the light changed, which earned me a honk. Grand-Pied turned around and spotted me before I could duck into a doorway.

"What do you want?" he growled.

"Just to talk to you. Can I buy you a drink?"

His eyebrows raised, making for a comical surprised expression on such a craggy face. "If you must."

Startled by his easy acquiescence, I blurted, "I don't want to keep you from doing what you were going to do. I'm not interrupting you, am I?"

"If you were so concerned about interrupting my afternoon, why would you be following me?"

"Good point."

He slowed his stride so I could keep up with him. "And I was going for a drink at the end of a long day. It's a normal thing do to."

I didn't hear the capital N in Normal, but his words reminded me of the trial he was supposedly undergoing. Could I help save him from the cult as well?

"It's not a cult, Doctor Gordon," he said.

"Did you just read my mind?"

"You're thinking loudly. Hasn't your Fae girlfriend taught you anything?"

Had Reine said she could read minds? I couldn't recall. "I don't know what you mean."

"That some creatures have better telepathic abilities than others."

I imagined shielding myself, and Grand-Pied nodded. "That's better. However, I should have warned you after I figured out what you want. Ah, here we are."

He opened the door of a bar with copper stills that sat in front of the windows, and the bouncer at the door waved us through the narrow entrance hallway. We walked up a flight of stairs covered in textured black rubber and into a light and airy room with green walls and blond wooden furniture. It reminded me for a second of Aolynn's castle in Faerie, and I caught myself looking around for the old woman whom I was pretty sure was the Lady of the Forest's ancestor, maybe the

First Lady herself. Then I recalled myself back to the time and place.

Grand-Pied regarded me with a new expression—curiosity. "You've had some interesting adventures, friend."

"You could definitely say that."

I attempted to pop my shields back up, but I feared I hadn't been quick enough considering that night in the castle had been the first time Reine and I had made love. The thought of her leaning over the balcony like an ice princess whose heart only I could thaw ran me through with alternating lusty heat and terrifying cold. Would we ever be able to see each other again outside of some alternate or dream world?

A hostess led us to a table for two by the window looking over one of the streets and across from some ornate government building.

Once she left, Grand-Pied read through the beer list and growled. "I've yet to find one that doesn't taste like deer piss."

"Try a Belgian. They're sweeter, maltier."

"All right..."

"I'll buy."

His lips twisted slightly upward—a smile? "Then definitely all right."

A young male server came by, and we both ordered the one Belgian style they had on tap and an appetizer, a plate of melted Brie with baguette and seasonal fruit.

Once the menus had been whisked away, Grand-Pied folded his massive hands in front of him and glared at me. Or maybe that was his friendly look. Hard to tell.

"Are you going to say why you've chased me down and are plying me with food and drink, Stoney?"

Was he teasing? Hades, it was hard to tell. If I were a mental health professional, I'd be noting, "restricted range of affect, as in almost none," in his chart.

"I have a couple of problems that I could use help with from someone of your particular talents."

His mouth twisted again, and this time I was pretty sure it wasn't a smile. "Sorry to tell you, but I don't do that stuff anymore."

"What stuff?" I couldn't resist asking.

"The walking. The telepathy, unless someone is rudely loud in their thinking. The other things that creatures like you couldn't fathom."

"Like changing the atmosphere of an entire realm?" The question escaped from my lips, and he stilled and tilted his head.

"Like that." But he didn't sound as sure, and I recalled that Lily had said he would find the problem intriguing.

I let him stew over that since I saw our food and drink approaching. The server brought our beers, and a young woman set the plate of Brie, bread, and apples on the table.

"Can I get you anything else?" Our server darted glances between the two of us, and I suspected he would prefer to be anywhere but there. Grand-Pied had that grumpy demeanor, and I likely emanated strong "go away" vibes as well.

"That's all for now," I said. "Thank you."

He bobbed his head and scurried off. Grand-Pied dipped a slice of bread into the melted cheese, chewed, swallowed, and said, "Let's say, hypothetically, that I would be willing to help you with the atmosphere problem. Which atmosphere, and what do you need to change about it?"

"The atmosphere in Faerie is poisonous for gargoyles. I almost died from being there for a few days."

"But you're in love with the queen."

He said it so matter-of-factly I wanted to shake him. "I'm not just in love with her. I love her. We're bonded, but even if we weren't, I'd move heaven and earth to be with her. If I could."

He picked up an apple and repeated his swipe-bite-swallow routine. I couldn't eat. Anxiety over what he could do and maybe *would* do danced through my gut and tied my esophagus into a merry little knot.

"And how long has the atmosphere been that way, hostile to you?"

"I don't know. At least several thousand years. No one remembers who altered it or why, only that the gargoyles and Fae used to be allies."

Another bite, another long pause. I bet his students wanted to throttle him sometimes.

"They did."

The two words dropped into the space between us with a silent explosion of possibility.

"You know what happened?"

He shook his shaggy head. "I didn't witness anything. I'm not that old. But I can tell you the change happened sometime around the Great Rising."

"So ten thousand years ago."

"Yes, just long enough for some species to have evolved for them to breathe the air as it is now, not as it was then."

"Is that long enough for a species to change significantly?"

"In Faerie it is. Time passes differently there in more ways than one."

Disappointment poked a hole in the bubble of hope that had grown around my heart, and I sat back and down as it deflated. "So if you were to change it, you would potentially make the atmosphere inhospitable to some of the creatures there."

"Yes. It would ruin their home."

"Hades," I muttered. I couldn't ask him to do that, to kill scores of innocent creatures just so I could shack up in the city of the light Fae with Reine.

Reine! "Even if you can't help me with the atmosphere problem, there is something else."

He drained the last of his beer and blinked at me. I took a bite of Brie and apple and signaled our server for another round even though I'd barely touched my beer.

"What? Another challenge? How could anything compare to changing all the air in a realm?" He shook his head. "You've got balls asking that, Stoney. I'll give you that."

"Thanks, I think. No, it's not that big, but just as important for me. Reine is stuck in a time loop. A trap someone set for her, I'm sure of it. She's looking for clues to unlock it and break out, but she's not having much luck."

"And if she doesn't figure it out soon, she'll be trapped forever?"

I spat the beer I'd just sipped back into the glass. "Is that what could happen?"

"That's how those traps work."

"Can you help us with that?"

He looked into his second glass of beer, which now lacked half the liquid it had come to the table with. "Maybe. That's an event of interdimensional significance, after all. The queen of Faerie being trapped."

"Yes! It could destabilize everything, all the realms." Somehow my first beer had gone empty, and I grabbed the second.

He rubbed his beard like a stereotypical professor type, and I tried not to giggle. "That may qualify as an emergency."

"I would say so. More than just for me."

"I shall consider it." He held up a hand before I could object. "If, that is, you buy us another round."

I ordered more beers and some wings, chicken fingers, and fries to soak it all up. He ordered a salad "for some vegetables so we could pretend to be healthy."

The words coming from him struck me as being hilarious,

or perhaps I had achieved giddy at the thought that he would help me. Or so I hoped.

When we walked out into the soft air of the humid summer night, we leaned on each other. I'd forgotten to warn him that Belgian beers had higher alcohol content, and somehow, I'd forgotten that I didn't drink much. The spell of the dimension-walker, maybe?

My phone rang, and I saw my mother was calling again. Thank gods. Perhaps she had some answers.

"Hello?"

"Lawrence, thank goddess! Look, wherever you are, get out of there and go somewhere safe."

"What do you mean?"

Sharp pain shot down my left arm, and I glanced down to see the feathered end of a dart sticking out of my biceps. "Hades," I muttered just as the world went black.

24

REINE

Lonna and Selene allowed me to have the bed, so I didn't have to sleep in the garden and risk our friend coming upon me unawares. They agreed to keep an eye out for him, and I heard them change in the main room. I listened in case the time bubble interfered like it had previously, and I had to change them back.

Selene went first, and when she answered Lonna's questions about who, what, and where she was, Lonna changed. Both moved quietly, and I allowed myself to exhale a relieved sigh that when they controlled their transformation, they kept their human brains as online as a lycanthrope could. As for what they'd do to our intruder, I suspected they'd corner him and bring him down if he dared to appear. What sort of experience did he have with werewolves? If he belonged to the Order of the Silver Arrow, not good ones. I'd implored Lonna and Selene to be careful—there was no telling what sort of weapons he carried.

Sleep took me with the speed of a falling black stage curtain, and I swore I heard it thump to the ground just before I opened my eyes.

A quick look around told me where I'd landed—1920s New Orleans. Sir Raleigh hadn't followed, which was fine. I didn't want him to get caught in a different time. A dingy film muted the colors and lines of the distinct architecture of the French Quarter, and I recalled that at this time, whores, bars, and gangsters had run the area. Not company I cared to keep, but also where I knew to look for the physician I needed.

A pioneer in plastic surgery, he'd developed a cure for severe scarring, or that's what he'd claimed... He'd looked at Rhys and shaken his head, saying that his problem was too old and too severe for him to do much good, but had still given Rhys a scar softener and said he'd take another look in a few weeks. When we'd returned, we'd found his clinic boarded up tight.

How soon after his escape had I landed? I found out when I turned the corner. The clinic was located on the ground floor of a building that would later be a boarding house, brothel, and then upscale hotel with more than its fair share of ghosts. A young woman pounded nails into a board anchored at the corner of a window. I must have landed between my two visits.

I didn't think she'd recognize me, but to be sure, I cast a glamour over myself so I'd appear to be a nondescript brunette with a mole on one cheek. "Hello, is this the clinic of Doctor Robichaux? I've heard he can help me with..." I touched the mole.

The young woman turned to me; she appeared vaguely familiar. Her Creole accent gave her words a soft edge of menace. "Don't try to mess with me, Madame le Fae. I can see through your illusion and know who and what you are."

So much for that. I kept the glamour in place in case anyone else wandered by. "Very well. And you are...?"

"I was Nurse Lain, until..."

"Until what...?" Now I remembered she'd worked for Robichaux.

She turned back to her boards. "None of your business, *cher*. You've caused enough trouble already."

"Please tell me what happened."

She glared over her shoulder. "One like you pleading? Not so high and mighty now, are you? Did the salve the doctor gave you cause your brother's face to melt off?"

"No, although that would have been an interesting change. It would have given me something to work with."

"Too bad."

Her dismissive attitude irked me, and I had to breathe into the prickly frustration that had sprouted in my chest. "Are you going to tell me what happened or not? I don't know how much time I have."

She shrugged. "I have all the time in the world."

"Because the clinic closed?"

Another shrug.

"Because the doctor died?" I recalled poor Bartholomew de Veers and his pox. Had something also happened to Doctor Robichaux?

She snorted. "That would have been the kinder thing. He's going to wish he had once the spells catch up to him."

"Is he ill?" At least she continued to speak, but the frustration had taken on a burning aura, and I feared I would lose my temper like I had with Lonna.

"No, he took the money you gave him and ran off. No telling where he ended up. I've got angry patients hounding me all the day and night, so that's why I'm boarding up this place. To tell them it's truly gone." Despair wafted off her in sickly sweet waves.

"Ugh, I'm so sorry that happened. What will you do?"

She didn't bother to shrug, only said, "I don't know. I've applied to the hospitals, to other offices, but Doctor Robichaux had a reputation, *savvy*? It's tainted me. Some blame me for him going missing."

I didn't bother to comment on how unfair that was. She already knew. "Is there anything I can do?"

"If you can give me some money…"

"I'm afraid I don't have any with me." And if I did, it would be printed much later than she'd lived. I didn't wear any jewelry to give her, either. "I'm sorry."

"That's what I thought. What he told me you'd say." She threw a fistful of nails at me so quickly I didn't have time to duck. The iron burned my skin, and I swatted it away as if it were stinging wasps.

"What was that for?"

A male voice answered from behind me. "To distract you."

I turned to see him throw two chains to the former nurse, both made of iron that hissed through the air, one on either side of me.

Electric panic spread from my hips, where the chains hovered, in both directions, through every nerve and blood vessel until I quivered with tingling fear. And underneath it, white rage. Before I could decide what spell to summon, they darted around me so I was well and truly caught.

I refused to show my fear. The iron dampened my magic, but I could still access some. I summoned my lasso, but it fizzled out. I also tried teleportation, and the scenery flickered but I didn't go anywhere.

Then the chains' hissing made sense—they'd been enchanted by a dark Fae. No doubt some traveled to and from the city, judging from the architecture I'd seen in the dark Fae capital.

My throat tightened to the point it wanted me to squeak, so I pitched my voice low and threatening. "Do you have any idea who I am? You've made a grave mistake."

They looked at each other and laughed. The man, whose stocky build and shoes matched the impressions I'd gotten of my garden stalker, grinned at me. "I've finally caught you, and now I'll be free. Release me from the time loop. Let me return to my own time, and I'll spare your life."

It took me a few seconds to sort through his words. "Wait. You're caught in the time loop?"

"Yes. Why do you think I keep popping up where you are? I've been tethered to that damn cottage or to you for hundreds of years."

"That would explain why you're so pissed. Look, Mister…"

"I'm not giving you my name, Fae."

"All right, I'll call you Mister Stalker. Look, Mister Stalker, we're in the same situation. Why don't we work together, and we can figure this out? Let me go, and I can help you."

He shook his head. "If I let you go, I'll continue to be stuck in this eternity of strange times and places or the horrible monotony of the cottage."

"What is all this about?" Lain gazed back and forth between the two of us. "You're talking gibberish. What is a time loop?"

"Nothing for you to worry about. Here." The man reached in a pocket and pulled out a gold coin. "This should take care of you for the future. Give me your ends of the chain."

The time bubble spell reached its icy tendrils into the humid day, and I welcomed its cool brush. It grasped me like a giant hand, but when it tugged, it slipped. My hands went transparent for a moment, but then they returned to their normal opaqueness.

And searing pain replaced the grip of the spell. It had made me disappear just enough for the chains to go from being wrapped around my body outside my clothes to inside them, and the sizzling of my flesh provided an undercurrent to my scream.

Lain dropped her chain and backed away, palms out. "What did you do to her? You said she wouldn't feel that much pain."

"It's the spell we're caught in. It tried to extract her, but it didn't take her because of the chains. Now they're touching her skin." He didn't sound upset. In fact, he continued with glee, "Take that, Fae bitch. Experience some of the pain I've known for the past two hundred years."

"Two hundred... What? I'm done." Lain left, and the man picked up her chain. He tugged, and the links dug deeper into my side.

The pain crested in a wave so painful it cut off speech and thought. I could only think about dying and wished for the blackness of unconsciousness. But some small part of me, that little place in my chest that connected to Lawrence, tugged at my dwindling consciousness.

Lawrence. If I died, he would, too.

What could I do? I reached deep into that well of magic, that box I kept hidden away with my forbidden Fae power. I could only manage a tiny spell, but it would have to be enough. I focused on two connected links of each chain and turned a sliver of the spot where one met the other into the first material I could think of—bread.

The chains whipped off me, tearing welts of fire and burning ice across my flesh. I fell to my knees, and the time loop spell scooped me up. When my back met the soil of Irina's garden, my body took a deep gulp of the earth energy, but before I could heal myself, I passed out.

25

LAWRENCE

I swam through blackness to the swirling consciousness of having been drugged and opened my eyes to the flower-patterned stippled ceiling of an apartment that had been built in the late twentieth century. My brain clicked back online with the thought that they really didn't make ceilings like they used to. The crown molding of the Georgian and Victorian eras had been the height of wasteful extravagance...

Wait, why was I thinking about ceilings?

A low rumbling caught my attention, Grand-Pied's deep voice.

"I didn't mean to get caught up in this matter," he was mumbling. "I don't want to be, but I have a responsibility. Or feel like I do."

A pause.

"What? Why would bringing him to his ladylove do that? Do you have no sense of compassion?"

Another pause. Who was he speaking with?

"No, I haven't used my powers as a dimension-walker in two years. And you should give me some credit for alerting you as to this problem, Grimm. I could have done what he needs without saying anything to you."

Yes, he was definitely on the phone, apparently talking to his dimension-walker handler, the charming Agent Grimm.

Touch came back next, and the sensation of a limb waking engulfed my entire body with prickly energy. What had that drug been? Something designed to immobilize, then torture, someone like me. Could a gargoyle sedative have been developed? It wouldn't surprise me, especially if a Fae had been involved.

Grand-Pied finished his call. I lay shaking, and the final tingles subsided, leaving me wracked and exhausted.

"Oh, good, you're awake." His tone hung somewhere between sarcastic and mildly enthused.

"Yes." I struggled to raise myself to my elbows, then to sit on his oversized couch. I wasn't a short gargoyle, but the over-stuffed navy-blue cushions almost swallowed me. "Did you see who did that to me?"

"No, they turned and ran off before I could see. I opted not to chase them so they couldn't take you."

"Thank you. I appreciate your wisdom and foresight." Indeed, he'd resisted doing what I would have done in the same situation, leaving my companion open to being whisked away when I gave chase.

"You're in over your head, gargoyle. Is that the price of living a paranormal life?"

"What? You think I'm living openly as a paranormal creature?" I snorted.

His brows made a confused V. "You generally reside in The Aerie with the others of your kind, do you not?"

"I do not. I live in Atlanta. I'm a veterinarian with the CPDC, so yes, I suppose I'm open there, but not in the rest of my life."

He sat on the ottoman in front of an armchair that also looked like it had been custom-built for him.

"Are you not, though? Your girlfriend, the Fae. She knows what you are."

"Yes..."

"Is there anyone you interact with regularly who doesn't? I'm not talking about people at the grocery store or other places."

I thought through my day-to-day interactions, or what they'd been before Reine had dropped into my life and stirred everything up. I'd gone to work, hung out mostly with my CPDC colleagues—grief stabbed through my chest when I recalled I'd never be able to do so again with Kestrel's parents, my best friends—and hadn't done much beyond that.

"I suppose not. But I can tell you that although we all knew what we were, whether gargoyle, witches, or shifters, we still lived a relatively normal life."

"How can you do that? You have to shift sometimes."

"Yes, but not often. And not in public, obviously." How long had it been since I'd taken a late-night flight around my neighborhood? A while. I couldn't remember the last time.

"You're lucky. You've surrounded yourself with others like you so you don't have to hide. So it's safe."

"Is that why you're joining the Normals? To be safe?"

He rose and crossed the room. He stood at his window and pulled the green curtain back to reveal a view of downtown Athens, at which he scowled. "You don't know what it's like to be hunted your entire life. For others to look at you with curiosity and horror."

I tried to rise, but my legs wouldn't let me yet. I rubbed my quads to bring some life back into them. "I do know what it's like to be hunted. Or to worry about it. My father was murdered in front of me because a Fae thought he'd had a hand in scarring the Fae's face."

Grand-Pied turned from the window. "That was your family?"

"You heard about that?"

"I know of The Aerie, remember? I've spoken to your mother, the queen. I didn't know you're a prince."

"I'm not. I don't claim to be, anyway."

My vision went monochrome for a second, and then some force scooped out my heart and replaced my blood with lava. I let out a scream before I clamped my mouth shut and wrapped my arms around myself with the whimper "Reine."

"What is it?" Grand-Pied knelt beside me and placed one of his hands on my head. The pain subsided, but like it sat on the other side of a piece of tissue paper and pressed through.

"Reine. Something's happening to her." I tried to stand, but I couldn't, and I plopped to the couch. "I have to help her. I have to get to her!"

Strength I didn't know I had bubbled up from somewhere in my solar plexus. I grabbed the front of Grand-Pied's polo shirt and brought his craggy face to mine. "I don't care about your trial or your Normals. The Fae queen's life is in danger, and I have to help her." Then words poured out of me I would never have thought on my own. "I am her sworn protector, and I deputize you."

The lights flickered, and my vision went monochrome again. Searing pain poured through my chest and whipped around my sides, then disappeared and left heavy weakness in its wake. I sagged back to the couch and blinked. The connection to Reine remained, although with the tenuous strength of a spiderweb strand. I buried my head in my hands. "Gods."

Grand-Pied stepped back. "I don't know what happened, but the entire fabric of this realm shook. A flag in the universal wind."

"The queen of Faerie is in danger. What would happen if she were to die?"

"The Queen Spell would find another, but only if there is

one who is worthy and is in the line of succession. Does your girlfriend have siblings? Children?"

It hurt to move the boulder of my tongue. "Only a brother that I know of, and no children." At least none in my awareness. I was pretty sure she would have told me...wouldn't she?

Grand-Pied rubbed the back of his left hand with his right one, and then stopped and held it up to the light. A vaguely familiar symbol had appeared, a bird-like rune. It reminded me of ones I'd seen somewhere in Faerie, but I couldn't dredge up where from the quicksand of my memory.

He pulled me up by my shirt, and my feet dangled over the floor like a broken puppet's. "What did you do to me, Gargoyle?"

"I don't know," I gurgled. "It just came out."

He dropped me, and I landed in a heap. I crawled toward the door, but he blocked my way. "No one should be able to mark one such as I without my consent."

The tingle of glee at his annoyance gave me the strength to stagger to my feet. "Well, maybe something bigger than you is at play here, Professor. And the sooner you help me, the sooner that mark will go away."

He growled, and I commanded, "Take me to Reine."

"All right, but only because whatever is going on with her will have far-reaching effects for the rest of her and your realm. And possibly mine." He clamped my arm in one giant hand, and his apartment disappeared.

26

DOSSIER: PRINCESS REINE

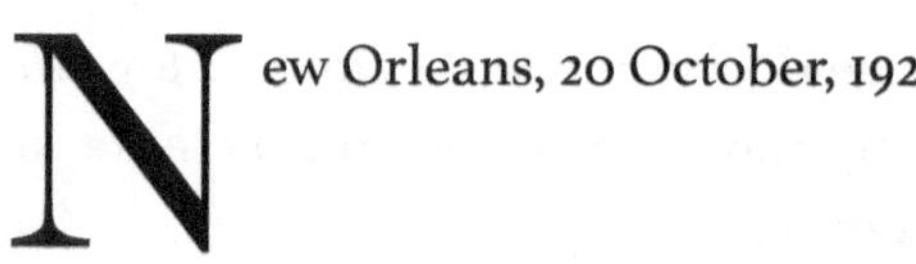

New Orleans, 20 October, 1921

REPORT BY SIR GERALD BRIGADINE, First Regiment of the Silver Arrow, Tracker Division

DEAR SIR or Madam or Respected Creature,

I write to you from a warm autumn day in New Orleans. Although I continue to be trapped in the time loop, I have learned to appreciate the comfortable days. I suspect my improved countenance also has something to do with progress in my quest to extract myself from the time loop.

Princess Reine and Prince Rhys have led me a merry chase, but finally they have brought me to a place of powerful magic and practitioners willing to trade their knowledge for the "antique" coins I carry. I am running low, but I suspect I shall not need my money, which has passed from common use now for over a hundred years, for long. Dollars, francs, pounds... They are at once familiar and novel to me, and I am bewildered by the paper money with no basis for trade. I believe the Templars may have tried such a thing in the olden days, but then what are the olden days?

Please forgive me. I am giddy.

Here is my report.

The two Fae visited a physician known in the relatively new field of reconstructive surgery, which has increased in need and use since the wars of the nineteenth century left so many disfigured and the hazards of city life have caused maiming to become an everyday occurrence. Once they left with yet another ointment I suspect will be of little use to them, I entered to find a young nurse at the front desk. I made up a reason for my visit to the doctor, and I convinced her to let me in without an appointment. She led me in, and I found in him the reincarnation of Bartholomew de Veers. I know not how this occurrence could be possible. Could the Fae be visiting the same physician or healer throughout time looking for their cure?

He did not recognize me and launched into the questions one would expect to be asked, which gave me the moments I needed to collect myself. But I could not take my eyes from him, and he confronted me with, "You're not here about your wrist and that old brand, are you? Do you have something to do with the two that just came in? They also had a strange air about them."

I nodded and apologized. "Forgive me, Doctor, but I am here for your good and not my own. Those two have been causing trouble for practitioners such as you for a long time, and I am here to warn you and give you a means of escape." I handed him my next to the last gold coin. "This plus whatever they paid you should enable you to escape and set up elsewhere."

I expected an argument, but I recalled that this person, this soul, had never had a family and had always been a loner. He nodded and pocketed the coin.

"You have my thanks...Gerald. Not Matthew Slater, as you told my nurse. How do I know your name?"

"I have helped you in the past, although you likely don't remember."

He shook his head. "No, I do not, but I trust you. Your words ring true." He left, and I did likewise.

My next stop was to a practitioner a few doors down from him. This one practiced more witchery than medicine, but that's what I needed to capture and destroy the Fae that continues to drag me through time.

I hope to give you my next report in person.

WITH HOPEFUL REGARDS,

GERALD BRIGADINE
  Your Loyal Tracker

27

LAWRENCE

The forest-printed wallpaper of Grand-Pied's apartment resolved into real trees, and my gargoyle earth and water senses picked up a few things about them in the seconds it took us to fully materialize in that place.

First, they were ancient, Like, true old growth forest, possibly cleared by the Romans but not likely, ancient.

Second, they hid many secrets, and the garden in which we stood had a certain impermanence to it.

Third, the earth energy had recently been depleted. I wrenched myself from Grand-Pied's grasp and turned to see why.

Two women, a tall brunette and a redhead, carried a limp Reine into a thatched cottage. I didn't recognize my wings had ripped through my shirt—although thankfully the rest of me hadn't changed—until I landed in front of them and gently took Reine in my own arms. She'd always been pale, but her skin appeared as of white porcelain, and her lips had faded from seashell pink to the faintest of tan.

"What happened?" I growled to the redhead Selene, whom I recognized. She'd accompanied Reine to Atlanta the first time.

She clasped her hands to her chest. "Lawrence, thank the gods. Lonna, this is Reine's mate."

The brunette eyed me with suspicion. I couldn't say I blamed her. "Well, that's convenient. What are you doing here, and do you know where to find Max and Gabriel?"

"The wizard and lycanthrope? No, I don't know where they are. Get out of my way."

I shoved past them into the cottage, and my wings disappeared so they wouldn't knock anything over. The cool air stung my now bare shoulder blades and my back through my tattered shirt, but I didn't care. Holding Reine this close filled me with a sickly purple energy that combined the rose-blush joy of reunited love and the deep blue terror of the ocean in a storm that roiled of potential loss.

Gods, I must be upset if I was getting poetic...

I had to focus beyond the thrill of finally holding her again and an undercurrent of pride for making it to her side to protect her. She held the earth force that I'd sensed had gotten sucked out of the garden, but she must have passed out before she could use it. I lifted her shirt to see what injuries had been done to her in the places I'd felt them. The lips of red welts sneered at me like she'd been flogged with iron. Some ancient sense told me someone had tried to fatally injure her and had almost succeeded.

I didn't know how to heal her, but instinct had carried me this far, indeed had been with me since our bond had informed me of her peril, and I held my hand over one sticky wound and focused on bringing the healing earth energy to it. It took some effort, but it worked, and the welt faded into nothingness, not even a scar. The next one came more easily in that I knew what I was doing, but it was so long I had to use both my hands pressed middle finger to palm.

"What are you doing?" That was Lonna, whom I'd pegged as the bossy one.

Grand-Pied responded, thankfully, so I didn't have to break my concentration too much. "He's healing her. The gargoyles were once the guardians of the Fae. The knowledge still resides in them somewhere." I imagined him rubbing the back of his hand.

"Can you help me?" I asked him over my shoulder. "She drew in the energy, but I don't have all the finesse I need to direct it."

"As your deputy, I suppose I must," he grumbled.

"Is that a…?" Selene asked. I guessed she'd never met a dimension-walker before.

With Grand-Pied's help, we got Reine's wounds healed, and I brushed her hair back from her forehead. "How long until she wakes?"

"I can't tell you, Gargoyle. She was gravely injured, especially for one of her kind."

"If I ever find out who did this…"

"Oh, I'm sure I can tell you," Selene spat.

"Who, then?" I wanted to wheel around and grab her, force her to tell me, but Reine's still face kept me anchored to the chair beside the bed.

Lonna stood on the other side behind Grand-Pied. "We don't know his name, only that he's been stalking us. Stalking her, rather."

"What does he look like?"

Selene frowned. "Nondescript, middle-aged guy. Graying black hair. Flat nose. Craggy face." She rubbed her arms. "The main thing that stands out about him is his desire to destroy her."

Grand-Pied rumbled an agreement and added, "Sounds like a Tracker."

"A what?"

"The vargamore Wolfsheim devoted a branch of the Order of the Silver Arrow to shadowing his enemies, finding them if necessary. The Trackers. He chose them specifically for their abilities to blend in."

"Good to know," Lonna said. "Does the Order still use them?"

"Possibly." Grand-Pied rose from his chair, and his head brushed the ceiling. "Ladies, perhaps we should give Lawrence some time."

"Thank you," I mouthed to him. He nodded, and his expression didn't change, but I'd like to think I saw a smile flicker over his lips.

I turned to Reine and brushed her hair back. Pain no longer poured through our bond, but neither did the emotions I'd become so accustomed to I almost didn't notice them.

I twined one of her curls around my finger, and Sir Raleigh jumped up on the bed. "I was wondering where you'd gotten to."

He gazed into my eyes, but he didn't speak, and I couldn't make out the message he tried to impart.

"I don't know if she'll be okay," I told him. "But I'm sure you can help."

He snuggled into the crook of her waist, and I returned my attention to her face. Thankfully she didn't have the waxen appearance of a corpse, but she still lay with unnerving stillness.

"Do fairy tale cures work on the Fae?" I asked before I leaned over and brushed her lips with mine, then lay my forehead against hers and closed my eyes. "Don't hold back from me. I want to feel what you feel, to dance in the rain even if it's cold and stings. I'm a gargoyle. We like that kind of thing." A storm brewed in the center of my chest, of fear and regret and the heaviness of the certainty that we couldn't be together like we both wanted. "I'm happy for any moments with you. I'd give anything to be in a real thunderstorm with you in a shelter by a lake."

"With disappearing clothes?" Her teasing whisper tickled my ears like vapor wisps, and I opened my eyes.

"Hey." I tried to back away, but she brought my mouth to hers, and this time we shared a real kiss. I had to pull back before I gave into what I wanted to do—claim her on this straw bed. "How do you feel? Do you need anything?"

She caressed Sir Raleigh's head, then traced the places where the chains had burned her. "It doesn't hurt."

"No, I healed you. With some help."

Her brows drew together. "That's unfamiliar energy. A dimension-walker? You found one?" She looked up at me with hope that made her even more breathtakingly beautiful.

"Yes, and he's here with me." I helped her to sit, then to swing her legs over the edge of the bed.

"So weak still," she grumbled. "Damn him."

"Do you know his name?"

She shook her head. "No, but I aim to learn and to curse him. More than he already is. He's stuck in this time loop, too. That's why he wants me dead."

"He seems to have underestimated you."

She shrugged, then winced. "Barely. There's still some deeper damage." She pushed my hands away. "Only a Fae healer can help. I'll be fine. Let's get us out of here."

"All right but stay. The others can come back in."

She glanced down at the bed behind her, then shuddered. "No, thanks. There are too many shadows in here. Let's go back out to the kitchen."

28

REINE

A dimension-walker! Lawrence found a dimension-walker. How? I didn't think they existed in the Earth Realm beyond occasional brief appearances to confuse humans.

I'd woken a few seconds before Lawrence kissed me, but I'd been enjoying his rom-com worthy speech. I couldn't wait to dance with him in the rain—in the real Earth rain, not whatever substitute this place offered.

I leaned on Lawrence as we walked into the kitchen, where even Lonna appeared happy to see me. Lawrence helped me into a chair and held my hand as I gazed at the creature who introduced himself as Professor Grand-Pied.

"I'm honored to meet you," I told him. "Thank you for coming to help me."

"The pleasure is mine, Your Highness. And I appreciate you remembering the old protocols."

"If you had come to me in Faerie, we would be throwing a feast in your honor."

I liked to think that Lonna, Selene, and Lawrence all

regarded him with extra respect, but he held out his massive hands.

"And I would refuse. I am not attached to the false honor that comes with age and the novelty of experience."

"I accept." I bowed my head. "But I would like to repay you for your kindness in healing me and in helping me to escape this time loop. Can we go ahead and get started on that second part? I know my companions are eager to return to their families and to the search for their loved ones."

Grand-Pied folded his hands, and dread crept through me on silent dead feet.

"I'm afraid it's not quite so simple, Your Highness. I can help the two lycanthropes and the gargoyle, but I'm afraid that you must unlock the puzzle of the time loop before you can be released."

"What?" I stood, and my wobbly legs made me plop back on to the chair. "But I haven't figured out...wait. It keeps showing me points at which I interfered in peoples' lives and accidentally changed their courses." I glanced around, but nothing changed. "How is that not the key?"

"I don't know, but it isn't." He bowed his head. "I am truly sorry."

Lawrence squeezed my shoulder. "It's all right. I'll stay here with her. We can figure it out together."

I wrapped his hand in mine. "It's not that simple, is it? I have to do this on my own."

"No!" Lawrence bent down so our eyes met. "I'm not going to almost lose you again."

"It's him!" Selene pointed to the window, through which the face of my tormentor leered at us. With a laugh, he turned and ran toward the woods.

"I'll take care of this," Lawrence growled. He dashed out of the door, and his wings appeared, although he didn't garg out completely. He'd learned a new trick.

The man disappeared through the side of the time bubble, and for the first time, it turned transparent. Shadowy figures lined the outside, and they held shackles big and thick enough to hold even a determined gargoyle. I rose and screamed, "Lawrence, no!"

But he disappeared through the barrier. I reached out to him, but the others held me back.

"Now you need to figure this out for good, Your Highness," Grand-Pied told me.

"Why didn't you stop him?" I demanded. "Couldn't you see what awaited him?"

"I am not allowed to interfere in interspecies conflicts."

"Then that means..." I sank to the chair. "Oh, gods, Maeve has him." The other puzzle pieces fell into place. "And probably Max and Gabriel, too. She knew I'd come here to help the two of you and somehow managed to infiltrate the Institute. Then she arranged the accident, knowing I'd come here and run right into her trap."

Grand-Pied intoned, "No one plays the long game like a Fae."

"We have to go," Lonna said. "I'm sorry, Reine, but we have to find out who the traitor is because then they can tell us where Max and Gabriel are."

Selene's gaze bounced between me and Lonna, so I took her hand. "Go. I'll figure my way out of this."

She nodded, and then she did something that surprised me —she hugged me. "Be careful."

"I will. You, too." Then I turned to Grand-Pied. "Thank you for helping me and them. I am in your debt."

"I will remember that." He took Lonna's and Selene's hands, and they disappeared, leaving me truly alone for the first time in days...or had it been weeks? I couldn't tell anymore.

Dark clouds gathered in the sky, and the shadows of the approaching storm raced across the floor of the cottage.

I walked outside as the first fat raindrops fell. They soaked me through with surprising warmth, and I suspected I knew where I'd find my final clue.

"All right," I told the spell. "Show me."

THIS TIME I didn't have to dream or test the boundaries of the time loop. The inside of the cottage faded into a gray sky mottled with clouds that turned the normally turquoise ocean to a sea of lead. Even the sand under my bare toes had dulled from blazing white to dun. I knew this place, but it wasn't what I remembered.

The spell spoke. "*You're in someone else's feelings.*"

"*Who?*" I sent back in secret conversation.

"*Walk along. You'll see.*"

I did as the spell instructed and soon saw another person approaching me. A young woman with red hair and freckled skin walked with her head down and her arms crossed, a picture of dejection. That would explain the sad filter over everything.

She must be a powerful witch to have this effect.

The recollection of the day hit me in the gut. I had been in Grenada for my medical school interview. That's where I'd met Max, and we'd become classmates. Since travel wore me out, I'd stayed on the island as I awaited the results and had borrowed space from a wind elemental who ran a bed and breakfast. I'd worked for her in exchange for room and board, and I hadn't minded. The menial tasks had made for a welcome distraction from the worry that I wouldn't get in, that I'd have to figure out some other way to cure Rhys besides becoming a doctor myself and learning the miracles of modern medicine.

The day I'd found out I'd gotten in, a strange storm had hit the island. It had come out of nowhere, and I'd thought it unusual but couldn't put my finger on why. Now I knew—it had been born of the sadness and disappointment radiating from this young witch.

"Hello," I said when she got close enough to hear me.

She jerked her head up, and her eyes went from the dusky gray of the sky to the normal clear blue green of the ocean. Then she narrowed them. "Have you come to torture me further, Fae?"

I held out my hands. "No. Why are you so sad? You're ruining the weather for everyone else."

She snorted, and a gust of cold wind blew both our hair in strange halos around our heads. "I've just learned my dearest dream is not to be."

An icy drop of "uh oh" dripped through my torso. "What is that?"

"I'd applied to the medical school on the island. It's my one chance to fulfill my dream of being a plastic surgeon for..."

"For...?" The drop rocketed into my throat and made a cold lump.

"Well, I can tell you since you're one of them. For the paranormal beings who have been injured or disfigured." She gazed over the ocean. "But now I have to go back."

"Go back to where?" I thought through the younger classes, and although I didn't recall everything from my time in school, I was sure I'd remember a powerful redheaded witch.

"Back to my mother's house. She made me promise to go back and take care of her if I didn't get in."

"Oh. It pains me to hear that. Are you an accomplished healer?"

"As much as one can be when untrained." She looked at her hands. "I've had some minor success, but I need more theory and knowledge to be truly effective." She returned her gaze to my face. "And the admissions clerk said that I would have gotten in, but a Scottish student with incredible credentials swooped in at the last moment and shoved me to the waiting list."

Now the certainty squeezed a spiral around my heart—this young woman could have performed the miracle I'd been hoping to do myself.

Had I thought about the possibility that a modern healer could help Rhys? Yes, but so far none had been successful. But if I'd waited a tad longer...

Another gust whipped the sand into a mini-cyclone, and it built into a pane of glass between us.

"What happened to you?" I asked, both afraid of the answer and knowing it would be part of my penance.

"I returned home and became a veterinarian after my mother died." She smiled. "It was good work, but I always felt like I'd missed my true calling, my chance to make a big difference. And then I got sick and died."

I couldn't speak through the icy fist that had lodged in my throat, so I told her in secret conversation, *"I'm so sorry. I didn't know."*

She disappeared, but the pane of glass and the stormy beach remained. Now it showed me the paths that the lives I'd encountered had taken. The witch we'd helped to escape from the mob ended up in Prague and married a young man who turned out to have been the one who gave Bartholomew de Veers the vampire pox after he himself had been turned. This young woman had been their descendant, as had the nurse in New Orleans.

I'd not only changed the course of a few lives, but I'd inadvertently steered a family to its destruction, or at least away from the path it would have taken. What potential had my search for a cure for my brother destroyed? It seemed fitting that I'd truly sabotaged myself in the end.

"I see it now," I told the spell. "I've possibly changed the path of the world itself, and I am ready to accept my punishment."

When the scene faded, it didn't reveal the walls of the cottage or its garden.

29

LAWRENCE

My wings emerged, and I took off after the running man. With the scientist part of my brain, I calculated the best angle to land on him to bring him to the ground and pin him so he wouldn't fight back.

The gargoyle in me roared with the intent to destroy the threat to my mate. Hot rage bubbled up from the cauldron of my gut and engulfed me in prickly heat to the point my vision turned infrared. I'd heard of people's vision going red with anger, but when it happened to me, a moment of surprise made me hesitate.

That cost me.

He ran into the woods, and I looked up to see the shimmering edge of the time bubble...and the trap that had been laid for me on the other side. I tried to twist and change direction, but that only made me spin through the barrier like a rock through plastic wrap, and I landed on my knees in old growth woods that mirrored those I'd just come through.

The air turned thick, and I gasped. My surroundings went from red to gray, and my wings disappeared. Somehow the gnarled trees and vines appeared more sinister, and I searched for the source of the sensation of being watched by a thousand different eyes.

"Welcome back, gargoyle." The smooth voice did nothing to soothe the panic that had replaced the anger.

"Maeve. It's not lovely to see you again."

She walked over to me and tilted my chin up. "Now, now, is that any way to greet your mother-in-law, or future one, assuming you and my daughter get out of this alive?"

I wanted to punch her, but my limbs sat leaden. "I'm in Faerie, aren't I?"

"Yes, you are. Isn't the fresh air bracing? So much better than the polluted atmosphere of Earth."

I tried to slow my breathing, to limit my lungs' exposure to the corrosive atmosphere. I suspected that since I'd had damage before, each exposure would be worse. Like Fae Fire, the doctor in The Aerie had told me. I thought I'd healed myself, but perhaps not.

"I should've guessed you were behind all this."

She laughed. "Oh, and there's much more to come. But meanwhile, I need to reward this gentleman who drew you out. Gerald?"

The man I'd chased emerged from behind a tree. The coward had hidden. He couldn't have known the extent of Maeve's power or how much I'd be handicapped.

"Yes, my queen?"

Her melodic laugh would have made anyone smile, but it hit my ears like a riff on a poorly tuned piano. "What do you wish most of anything?"

"To escape from this time loop and have the life I missed."

She grinned, and I wanted to shout in warning, but the finality of what had already been done clogged my throat. She placed one hand on Gerald's head.

"Then so be it. You are released from the time loop. Unfortunately, it's the only thing that kept you alive for hundreds of years."

His thick features turned into a mask of terror, then pain, and he tried to jerk back. I couldn't look away as his hair went from gray to white, then disappeared. Wrinkles crawled down his face and neck and into his clothes until he shriveled like a formerly juicy fruit in the sun. Then his skin turned to dust and ash.

The last thing to go were his eyes, which remained locked on mine until even his bones crumbled, and he lay in a heap of clothes and dirt on the forest floor. The ground opened to swallow him.

I remembered to breathe, but the air had gone liquid with the terror of what I'd just witnessed, and my diaphragm would only move a millimeter. Did she have similar plans for me? For Reine?

Maeve dusted her hands. "Now that that's done... Why the horror, gargoyle? He tormented and attempted to kill my daughter. I couldn't allow him to go unpunished...for attempting to steal my satisfaction."

"You're the monster," I gasped out.

"And you're ever the chivalrous gargoyle. There, there, we'll make sure you're comfortable. Rhys?"

Another dart flew through the air and struck my shoulder. My bones turned to jelly, and I crumpled from my knees the rest of the way to the ground. The air suffocated me along with the pain that Reine's brother had once again betrayed her.

WHEN I WOKE, I found myself on the floor of a cell. My vision had gone gray again... No, that was the color of everything around me. Gray stone floors, iron gray bars, gray gloom that stretched as far as I could see down the hall...

"I think he's awake." The accent spoke of the Caribbean, the exact opposite of the colors and stagnant chill I found myself in.

"About time." That was a classic Scottish grumble.

I twisted and rolled myself to my side, then to a seated position against the wall, like the end of the worst yoga class ever. "Doctor Fortuna, Investigator McCord, there are many people looking for you."

My neck protested when I twisted my head, but I found the other men in cells, one on each side of me.

"Well, they're not doing a great job." Gabriel paced in his small space. "We've been here for, what, a week?"

Max lounged on the floor of his cell. He'd managed to make a sort of pillow from the blanket and straw they'd given us for bedding. "Something like that. Time moves differently here. Did you see Lonna? Abby?"

"Lonna, yes. She's doing as well as can be expected. She got caught in a time loop but is now released. So is Selene."

Gabriel stopped pacing and exhaled. "Thank gods." He resumed his back-and-forth stomping.

Had he been so worried he'd been afraid to ask about his fiancée? Or did he, like me, battle his inner creature, in his case a wolf, to maintain control in these threatening circumstances?

"Do you know how they got stuck in one?" Max asked. "Was it another trap?"

"Yes, by Maeve to catch Reine. She happened to net the other two as well, which was good since Reine ended up in a bit over her head." Shame engulfed me in a cold, prickly wave. "And I left her to fend for herself."

Max nodded with a rueful half-grin. "All part of her plan, I imagine. No one plays the long game like a Fae."

My lips twitched with a smile of recognition that he, too, had used the expression. And then I grimaced at the thought that although we'd all said it, none of us had truly appreciated the ramifications. "Have you performed any spells to figure out what's going on or how we can get out?"

Max's shoulders twitched like he was too exhausted to manage a full sigh. "I'm limited in what I can do here. The prison appears to be magic-proof. Gabriel can't change, which has been torture because it's a full moon, has been since we arrived."

Horror and sympathy twisted around my heart at the thought of not being able to shift when compelled. "Gods. I'm sorry." Thankfully we gargoyles didn't have that need, although the opposite—putting off shifting too long in either direction—could also result in bad things. I dared not think what.

Gabriel waved his hand. "Don't talk to me. I have to pace to focus on not exploding. I don't know how much longer I can hold on."

"Understood. Max, how did y'all end up here?"

The corners of Max's eyes crinkled. "Y'all? You have lived in the South for a bit, haven't you?"

"You don't have to talk if it's too tiring."

"No, no, it's fine. Perhaps we can put our stories together and figure out the key to escaping this hell. From what I understand, a Fae named Ellerin approached Gabriel and told him he'd be disappearing for a while to 'go underground,' and asked him to get a message to Reine that more things are afoot from an old enemy. Is that correct, Gabriel?"

The werewolf nodded.

"He and I decided to engage in our own investigation and dug through some of the history of the area going back before Lycan Castle. You may be aware that the countryside is dotted with old castles, including Lycan Castle, the seat of the Werewolf Council? We found an entrance to a secret passage in the dungeon."

"That you hadn't noticed before? That they hadn't?" I raised my eyebrows, which felt like they each weighed five pounds.

What sort of energy must Gabriel be expending to move so much in that place?

"Yes." Max's cheeks turned pink. "But we didn't go in. We knew better."

"Then what happened?"

"Gabriel shifted, smelled the door and first few feet of the passageway, and we searched the surrounding woods to find the other end. Which we did. We thought it would be smarter to go that way than from Lycan Castle and surprise anyone who waited for us from behind."

"All right. But what did that have to do with Ellerin?"

"Gabriel smelled a hint of Fae magic and thought that was where he'd gone."

I leaned my head back against the stone. "And why did the two of you think it would be a good idea to try to follow him?"

They exchanged regretful looks, and Max replied, "It made sense at the time. At this point, I can only conclude we'd been put under some sort of Fae spell, a mild one so we wouldn't sense it, but powerful enough to draw us to seeking and finding the tunnel."

"Like in the Goblin Market poem." The literary reference surprised me, but it had captured my attention in the nineteenth century as part of my own investigation into my father's murder at the hands of... "Rhys! Have either of you seen Reine's brother Rhys lately?"

Gabriel scowled. "Not since I took out Wolfsheim."

"Maeve told him to shoot me with the tranquilizer dart that landed me here. So he didn't put me in the cell?"

"No, but our jailers are invisible. Food and water appear from time to time, as do clean bedding and empty buckets, but we never see anyone."

That gave me some relief. Fae couldn't lie, but it was possible that another Rhys, perhaps a human or some other paranormal creature, had wielded the dart gun.

The faintest of lines appeared between Max's strawberry blond brows and over his glasses. "Are you all right, Lawrence? You sound like you're having trouble breathing."

"Thank you for your concern, Dr. Fortuna. I can't talk much more, I fear." Indeed, invisible fists squeezed my lungs tighter with every word.

"That's all right. We need to get you out of here."

"We need to get ourselves out of here," Gabriel growled.

"Agreed. We know that Maeve captured Lawrence, and signs point to her involvement, especially after what Ellerin said. But to what end? What game is she playing?"

Gabriel stopped pacing and turned to face us. His eyes had gone wolf yellow, and his voice took on the timbre of a movie werewolf. "Don't you see the connection? Reine called me when the soul-eater broke into her house. She has a long relationship with you, Max. And Lawrence here is her lover. We were never the point. Maeve has collected us to force Reine into something."

The truth of his words poured through me in an icy deluge, and I closed my eyes. I'd hoped she had captured me to hurt Reine and the others to get them out of her way, but that would be too uncomplicated. We had all become pawns on Maeve's board, and I dreaded to think what Reine would be willing to do to save us, the three non-Fae creatures she cared most about aside from Sir Raleigh, who had proved to be smarter than all of us.

That left me with one question—where in Hades was Ellerin?

30

REINE

I found myself in the familiar gardens of the palace of the light Fae. I sank to my knees in relief at physically being there, not merely a dream projection, and buried my fingers in the grass. Sir Raleigh twined around my legs, and I picked him up and smooched him on the top of his head. He gave me that "how dare you do something as undignified as kiss me?" look familiar to feline companions and wriggled out of my arms. He stretched, first back with butt and tail up, then with tail and legs back and one arm reaching forward.

"It's good to be home, isn't it?" I stood, took one more sniff of the growing green grass and fresh flower scent, then brushed my hands together. I had a gargoyle to rescue. The fear of Lawrence being in Maeve's hands—for who else would be willing to ally with shadows?—fought in my brain with the knowledge that I had interfered with my own path and goals, leading me here, to a romance with a gargoyle whom I could never be with because Faerie was my home, and it would kill him.

If Maeve didn't do so first.

I walked toward the entrance of the palace, but Sir Raleigh blocked me.

"All right, where do we need to go?"

He turned to the right, and we climbed the steps leading from the garden to the palace patio, which added distance between us and the palace door. But we didn't turn back there. No, he led me to the rectangle of stone that led down to the catacombs.

I backed away. "I just escaped a situation where my life was in danger. I don't want to go down there."

He looked back and forth between me and the slab, and I got the message—no avoiding this trip to the underworld.

"All right. It's past time for me to visit Grandmother Tatiana's tomb, anyway. Perhaps she has some wisdom for me."

I approached the slab, and it disappeared to give me access to the catacombs beneath. Only a queen or queen-to-be and the highest-ranking light male Fae could open it, so that gave me some comfort. At least I hadn't lost my title to Maeve yet, although I had no doubt she would yank it from me in a heartbeat. And trap me in the catacombs forever.

That thought made a shiver slither from the base of my skull to my tail bone. I took a deep breath and descended. Sir Raleigh followed.

Once the daylight from overhead faded, I prepared to whisper the spell that would light the torch at the bottom of the stairs but found it already lit, as were the ones beyond. All right, that was strange.

"Hello?" I called. My voice echoed through the stone corridors, then faded into the inky silence.

Sir Raleigh pushed between my legs and led me on to the royal chamber, a large sarcophagus-like space with fluted columns and statues flanking the door. Each time I came down, some new aspect of the sculpture revealed itself. The first time, the figures had appeared as though they'd been made of wax and then melted. The second time, for my grandmother's funeral, the wings had taken on more detail, and I could tell they were different. This time the wings had become fully defined under the hand of the invisible sculptor, revealing the figure to the left as being a gargoyle with bat wings and two lumps on the still-misshapen head that could be turning into horns, and the figure on the right a Fae with the classic feathered wings, not the butterfly ones my flying form sported. The difference between the Fae statue and myself cracked my heart with sadness, although I couldn't say why.

The door to the tomb space disappeared, and Sir Raleigh and I walked under the lintel to find both the pool of black water that flowed in a constant whispered rush over one edge and into the ground below and a campsite. A bed roll laid folded in the far corner, and a lamp and a pile of books sat neatly beside it. A hint of savory tinged the typical icy water and dry-stone scents of the place.

I looked down at Sir Raleigh, who had gone over to sniff the objects. "Creepy place for a campsite. Surely we have better in the realm."

A male voice made me whirl around. "That's only for those who aren't fugitives in their own world."

"Ellerin!" I ran into his arms, and he gave me a big hug. Fae didn't typically put much stock in physical touch, but I'd come to relish it during my time in the Earth realm, and my eyes prickled. I wouldn't allow myself to cry, though. That would be weakness, and I already felt hollowed out from what I'd seen and experienced.

I pulled back, and he held me at arm's length and looked at me for a full minute.

"What is it?"

"You look good for having just come through a time loop trap. How did you make it out?"

I stepped away and rubbed my arms as the chill of the

memories and the space teased bumps from them. At my wish, a faux leather jacket appeared, and I put it on.

"I had to figure out the key to solving the puzzle of why someone had set the trap and what I needed to learn."

"I know. And I wish I could have helped you, but..." He shrugged. "I couldn't get to you and had to seek my own answers here about what your mother has been doing."

"I definitely want to know that, but..." Now I felt hot, so I removed the jacket. "It was a hard lesson."

"Most of the time they are. That's why those spells are so effective—the key is usually the thing that the one who's trapped doesn't want to admit to anyone, least of all themselves."

"That is definitely the truth."

He walked to the corner and sat on the folded bedroll. Sir Raleigh jumped on to his lap, and they looked at each other for a minute. I wished I could overhear their conversation, but I suspected the grimalkin was doing what he'd always done—reporting to the Fae who had called him into existence.

Ellerin nodded, and Sir Raleigh jumped down. Ellerin released a sigh. "Daughter, I wouldn't normally ask you to tell me now. I'd rather wait until you've had time to process, as the humans like to say, and confide in me, but I suspect that what you learned and what I've discovered are related."

I lowered myself to the edge of the pool, and Sir Raleigh hopped up beside me. "He knew you were down here, didn't he?"

"He suspected. He couldn't find me, so he went to Lawrence. I'm guessing the gargoyle found a way to you?"

"Yes." I scratched Sir Raleigh behind the ears. "In my dreams. And then he found an ally. But what has Maeve been doing?"

"First tell me the lesson you learned."

Sir Raleigh crawled into my lap and purred, and as always, I found the sound and sensation to be soothing. I stroked him as I spoke. "In my efforts to help Rhys, to heal him so we would be allowed into Faerie, I changed the course of not only individuals, but an entire family's history. It would have worked, too, but in the end, I sabotaged my goal." I gazed down at the grimalkin, who'd turned his face up to me in eyes-closed bliss. "I am a terrible person. I didn't even think about how my presence would impact others, but I should have known after that first time, when the poor witch had to flee her community because they caught her doing a spell for us. And I'm a terrible Fae because I care."

"Your caring makes you a good person. What human do you know without mistakes?"

"That's the thing. Only the evilest of humans have intentionally destroyed another's life, much less an entire family."

We sat in silence for a few minutes. Sir Raleigh's purr blended with the hushed dance of the water.

Ellerin brushed a hand over his short-cropped gray and brown hair. Was it grayer than the last time I'd seen him?

"I'm afraid, then, that Maeve knows and has been gathering evidence of this interference."

"This is what you've found in your investigation?"

"Yes, I've been searching through secret archives and talking to my contacts in this and the Earth Realm. She's attempting to gather enough evidence to prove that you've interfered with other realms' history enough that you deserve to be stripped of the throne...and worse."

"How is she getting the evidence?"

Ellerin stood and walked to the end of the room and back. I watched him pace but didn't say anything to let him gather his thoughts. That made me wonder what sort of lie of omission he was about to commit.

"When your grandmother Tatiana refused to ally with the vargamore Wolfsheim, Maeve went and made a backdoor deal.

She would help him where she could, and he would ensure your exile and have the Order of the Silver Arrow spy on you through your long life. They couldn't make you do anything, but they could attempt to obstruct you, especially if you were to loop back around to the places and times you'd been in."

"That was the spy. There was a man caught in the time loop as well. He tried to kill me to escape." I pressed a hand to where the worst cut had been. I definitely owed Lawrence and Grand-Pied a big favor for their healing.

"He sent letters back to the Order even though he couldn't escape." He stopped pacing and placed both his palms flat on the pool's rim. "I'm afraid they may have enough, Reine." He looked up. "You can't stay here, but I can help you escape, to hide. There are other realms where we can survive besides here and Earth."

The sadness that had cracked my heart earlier now caused my soul to crumble in grief. I'd never see Lawrence again, because I couldn't ask him to give up being there for Kestrel. "But what about Faerie? Who will lead?"

He smiled. "That you thought about your responsibilities before your mate speaks to me of your priorities."

I opted to continue my own lie of omission. I still couldn't find his in what he'd revealed. "I mean, Basil, Rhys, and you are doing a great job. Why would they go to Maeve?"

"Because she is the one they know of the queen's line. There hasn't been another who's heard or felt the Queen Spell, although believe me, since you've been gone, many have tried to evoke it."

"I'm sure."

"And do you know whether we've been effective? The realm is under more threat than ever before, and that also has people scared. In times of uncertainty, they turn to the familiar, even if it's horribly flawed."

I rubbed Sir Raleigh's soft ear. "That's very human of them."

"They have more in common with humans than they'd ever admit."

"So those are my choices—face whatever Maeve has ready for me or try to escape?"

"That's about it."

I returned my gaze to him. "'About it?' Is there another way?"

"If you die, the Queen Spell will be forced to choose another. Since it passed over Maeve, it will likely not return to her."

I closed my eyes. I'd been faced with my death in The Aerie, but at that point, it had been despair generated by a witch tugging on my insecurities and weaknesses.

If I were to choose my death now, it would be for the sake of my people, but what pain would it cause? Plus, I'd kill Lawrence, which was so not an option, and run away in a different sense. If I didn't want to abandon my throne and escape, and I couldn't abandon my life because as long as I still drew breath in some sense, I could still figure this out and perhaps accomplish something no other Fae had—make amends for screwing with human lives.

And no one would accuse me of abandoning my people...or Lawrence.

I opened my eyes. "I've made my choice."

A hole in the wall glowed with a cold blue light, and when I read the inscription over it, I almost convulsed in a full-body shiver. The name on the top of the tomb was my own.

"Then may the gods go with you. Unfortunately, we can't. But Reine?"

"Yes."

He hugged me again. "Don't let her get to you. Keep your head. In all senses. That's the only way you're going to make it through this."

"Thanks." I squeezed him one more time and released him.

Sir Raleigh gave me one last head butt, and this time I allowed the tears to come when I scratched his velvety head and ran my hand down his body. "Go take care of Lawrence," I whispered.

The glowing rectangle expanded into a doorway, and after one last glance at the grim-faced Ellerin and droopy-eared Sir Raleigh, I stepped through.

31

REINE

I stepped into a room that I had rarely been in before—the palace court chamber. I cast back to my memories and vaguely recalled a trial or two from my time before the exile. Only the nobility were tried in this room, as lesser Fae were issued punishment without opportunity for defense or argument.

The judge, whom I recognized as the senior Fae on the Queen's Council, sat behind a bench of white birch. His face had gone from youthful to ageless, and gray tinged the temples of his otherwise dark brown hair. I guessed that the judge's bench in the dark Fae castle—if they even had a courtroom— was made of ebony. The intricate marble pattern of the floor imitated the swirls of sunlight through clear shallow water, and the benches and barriers were of golden or other light-colored wood.

It would have been a cheerful place if not for the pending thunderstorm static in the air.

When I walked in, all who were present, which included the Council and much of the nobility, turned toward me. I thought I'd mentally readied myself since deciding to face

Maeve in this space. Nothing could have prepared me for the cold hostility that greeted me.

"It's about time you got here," Maeve drawled.

"I would think that someone as good as you are at time manipulation would have been able to figure out a way to not have these lovely Fae wait." All right, so I'd forgotten Ellerin's advice about not letting her get to me. I resolved to do better.

She looked up at the ornate blue and gold clock on the wall. "You have twenty minutes with your counsel before the trial begins."

"And who might that be?"

"Me." Basil stood from the front row on the right, and although the first shred of hope I'd felt since choosing this course attempted to unfurl in my chest, his facial expression told me I would be getting a pointed earful when we were alone.

Indeed, after the guard had shown us into an office to the side, he buried his head in his hands. "I can't be your counsel and your researcher and your regent, Your Highness."

"Where's Rhys?"

"Who the Hades knows?" He swept his arms out in a wide gesture. "I haven't seen him in a week, since you came to me from the time loop."

"Has it already been a week?" Hades, how long had Lonna and Selene been gone from the Earth realm, then?

"Something like that. Long enough."

"When did you find out about the trial?"

"This morning."

That would have been when I'd figured out the key to escaping the time loop. Maeve must have had everything in place, though.

I put on my bravest smile. "What's our plan, Counsel?"

He didn't reciprocate the expression. He walked around the desk and opened the folder on top to reveal a stack of old letters. "This is the evidence against you. You've been followed through your entire life by a spy named Gerald Brigadine." He handed me a sketch. "Does he look familiar?"

I had to take a deep breath and tell my rabbit heart to slow down. This man wouldn't hurt me again. "Yes. He was stuck in the time loop." I handed the picture back to him. "He tried to kill me."

"Good." He jotted something in a leather notebook. "That may help to discredit him. Where is he now?"

"Lawrence chased him out of the time loop. Basil, guess what I found out?" I couldn't help my excitement at sharing the news with my fellow nerdy Fae. "Dimension-walkers exist!"

He glanced up, and the corner of his full lips twitched. "Great. Do you know if they'd like to be a witness for you? Also, you'd better hope that Lawrence didn't kill this Brigadine guy. You're going to need him."

"I don't know. I haven't seen Lawrence since it happened."

"We're going to need character witnesses. Do you know of any we can call up quickly?"

"In ten minutes or less? No." Maybe not in longer. Lawrence and his family couldn't come to Faerie. I'd attacked Lonna and guessed she still smarted from it. Selene had also seen me at my worst. Max and Gabriel were missing. I didn't want to bring Veronica Chalice, who managed my store in Lycan Village, into this mess, and she could get me in more trouble for "interfering" with human commerce. And I didn't know how to get a hold of Barton Lucia or anyone else in The Aerie. Still, I suggested, "Barton Lucia may be a possibility. He's a physician and a Truth Seeker."

Basil drew a decisive line through the *Barto-* he'd started to write. "No Truth-Seekers. We're about to be in enough trouble with them."

"Why?"

"Because revenants have been escaping into the Earth

realm. So far, they've only frightened a bunch of animals, but it won't be long before they start attacking."

"How are they getting out?"

He put down his quill. "How the hell should I know? I've been tied up with other things, and I've only started receiving the reports in the past few days." He rubbed his eyes. "I'm sorry, Your Highness."

I placed my hand on his shoulder. "No, I'm sorry. I've relied on you too heavily, especially with Ellerin gone and Rhys..." I sighed. "Who knows where my useless brother has gotten off to?"

"No one as far as I can tell." He squeezed my hand, then pushed it off. "Well, this will have to be enough. You know your chances don't look good, right?"

"Yes." I swallowed the anxiety that threatened to swirl into panic in my gut. "The fact that you, a dark Fae prince, are my counsel speaks volumes about how reluctant my own people are to defend me. But we'll have to do the best we can, and I appreciate your willingness to help."

"That's all we can hope for. And you know that although I'm a dark Fae, I still serve you without hesitation."

His eyes held the intensity that sometimes made me uncomfortable and reminded me that he would like to be my consort.

But hearts, like Fae plots, couldn't be untangled, and Lawrence and I were about as connected as we could get. In fact, the aching in my chest had only grown since he'd flown out of the time bubble that morning, and I again had to quash my fears for his safety. I couldn't help him if I landed in Fae prison...or worse.

"Let's get this over with."

~

Whenever I look back on the trial, I'm not sure of the order anymore. I think it progressed in the way I'm about to tell it, but if time moves strangely in Faerie, then it hops and wiggles more in the realm of memory.

I walked into the courtroom with my head held at a regal angle. Thankful that Fae don't perspire, at least not much, I refused to allow those present to see how much they ruffled me. I didn't look at Maeve when I took my seat, and Basil sat toward the aisle, so he blocked her from my view.

Judge Stuffypants—my mind wouldn't catch on the names of the elder Fae who had formerly been my allies—banged his gavel and intoned, "The prosecution may make their opening remarks."

Maeve's counsel, a squirrely Fae who took care of the archives scooted his chair back, but she grabbed his shoulder before he could rise.

"I hope the court will indulge a mother's desire to address her daughter."

The judge didn't appear surprised by her request, and Basil and I exchanged worried glances.

"Go ahead, Princess."

She stood and emerged from behind their table. She walked to the center and bowed to the judge, then nodded to the audience and Council, who were to serve as the jury, before fixing her blue gaze on me.

"From the time you were little, you were always a handful." Her reminiscing tone held a warning, and I braced my feet against the floor in anticipation of the cyclone sure to come. "And I humored you, as did your father. In fact, that you know your father is a sign of how we coddled you since our harem system is designed to keep any one Fae from gaining too much influence."

Basil raised his hand. "Objection!"

"What is it?" the judge snapped.

"Queen Reine didn't find out who her father was until recently."

"Is that true, Your Highness?"

"Yes, your honor."

"Objection sustained. And while we can't lie, may I remind you that this court does not condone half-truths or deceptive language."

Maeve didn't let that slow her down. She dismissed the interruption with a wave of her hand. "Very well, Your Honor. Need I remind you, daughter, that your lack of responsibility led to your brother's disfigurement? You should have been with him, and yet you were off doing your own thing in direct contradiction to your grandmother's orders. And now, you dare to appear in this court, the first time you've spent any significant time in Faerie since our argument."

I would hardly call a magic battle that resulted in her being crushed by an elemental tidal wave an argument, but I shook my head when Basil asked me in secret conversation, "*Do you want me to object again?*"

"No secret conversation, Counsel," the judge snapped.

"Yes, Your Honor. However, I am wondering what Princess Maeve's address to her daughter has to do with the matter at hand."

I almost banged my head on the table. He'd just played right into her trap.

"It has everything to do with it, Counsel. My daughter has a long history of selfishness and lack of attending to her obligations. In fact, she's been shacking up, as the humans say, with her gargoyle lover in the Earth realm and ignoring the mounting problems we have here like the Great Rising. Rather than making allies with those we need to unify with like Queen Desdemona and her court, she has been gallivanting with gargoyles, whom as we all know cannot survive here."

The judge frowned. "Is that true, Your Highness? What is she not telling us?"

"That I am working on a solution to the issue of gargoyles not being able to breathe here, Your Honor. They are our best chance in defending against the revenants. If you recall your history, they were once our guardians."

Maeve laughed. "So you're pursuing a solution that would require someone powerful enough to change the entire atmosphere of Faerie, of which there are few, including the one who was killed during her encounter with you, the ice witch Grylja."

"That was Rhys," I argued. "I didn't want to hurt her."

"But you didn't act quickly enough!" She spread her arms in an "aha!" gesture. "As you can see, Council, my daughter lacks the decisiveness required of a queen."

Basil's hand shot up. "Again, not the matter that's on trial, so I must object."

"Your dark Fae counsel is quick to your defense," Maeve sneered.

The judge hit the pad with the gavel. "Sustained. Please sit down, Princess."

Maeve smirked at me, then resumed her seat. If the atmosphere in the courtroom had been cool before, now it prickled with hostility, and I could almost see the tatters of my reputation blowing in a doom-laden breeze.

Her counsel gave his opening arguments, and I massaged my sternum to dislodge yet another sting of betrayal. I'd thought the archivist and I had gotten along well, but I supposed he, like many of the Fae, had decided to ally with the one they thought would win, not necessarily who was right.

He gave the court information that I had just spent several days inadvertently reviewing, about how in my efforts to help Rhys, I had altered the course of a family's destiny to the point of keeping a promising young mind from becoming a physician that could help those like us in the Earth Realm. They didn't call Gerald Brigadine, and Basil and I side-eyed each other and the other table. What had happened to Gerald? Had they decided not to call him out of worry that we would attempt to twist his testimony to our advantage?

They did call up Aoine, the Lady of the Forest, whose green gowns simultaneously complemented and clashed with the decor of the courtroom.

"And what can you tell us of Queen Reine's activities in the Earth Realm?"

"I can't say anything about those, but I do know she and her party fled my castle in the middle of the night after I threw a ball for her." She dabbed the corners of her eyes with a silk cloth. "It broke my heart that she so cruelly rejected my opening my home to her."

The Fae in the courtroom all gasped at the breach of hospitality I had allegedly committed. In truth, we'd fled because we were in danger since I wouldn't join Aoine in her treasonous intentions against my grandmother.

Basil had been there and raised his hand, but the judge waved away the objection. "Do you have anything *relevant* to add, milady?"

"Obviously she spent so much time in the Earth Realm that she's forgotten how to be a Fae."

"You may go, Lady Aoine." The judge rubbed his temple with the handle of his gavel, and I had to admit that calling her had been strategic for Maeve. She must have anticipated that Aoine would be sent away after her irrelevant testimony and not give me any chance to argue against her accusations since they had nothing to do with the reason for the trial. But they would stick in the judge and Council's memory.

The prosecution didn't call me, but I knew they'd examine me at the end of the trial. Basil called a few witnesses including the king of the Winter Gnomes, who gave a lukewarm assessment of my character, a couple of minor Fae who remembered me from childhood, and Rhys, who had been the only witness to my actions since most of the humans involved had passed on or were missing. He didn't appear, of course. Where was he?

Finally, they called me to the stand, and I swore on an obsidian crystal that I would refrain from using deceptive language and that I would answer questions to the best of my ability.

The archivist came to stand in front of me. "Should've given me help for the library," he mumbled.

"You shouldn't have attacked Kestrel," I whispered back.

"Please share with the entire courtroom," the judge commanded. "Whatever personal squabbles you have don't have a place here."

"Were you present at all the points in time that were outlined in the first exhibit?" He pointed his stick at a list of times and places when Rhys and I had sought help from the various healers and medical professionals.

I opted to go for the simple approach so as not to give him any opportunity to twist my language. "Yes."

"And were you aware that your very presence in these people's lives could—not would, could—alter them irrevocably?"

That made me pause, and I decided to answer truthfully. "I honestly didn't think about it. I was in exile and moving through the world as I was forced to."

"'Forced to?' Did anyone force you to seek out healing for your brother's disfigurement?"

"No, but he's my brother. His injury pained him for a long time after, and even when it didn't, it restricted his facial mobility. I did what anyone would have done."

"So you've contradicted yourself. Were you forced to interact with anyone during your time in the Earth Realm?"

"No, but I was also not forbidden from it."

"It seems to me like you took advantage of your exile to advance your own position and wealth. Is it true that you built up quite a bit of money and resources and had a nice house near Lycan Village?"

"I lived frugally, worked as a healer, and was smart with the money I was given."

"By whom?"

"Presumably my grandmother."

"And mother?"

"She wasn't the queen, so she didn't control the resources."

"But she could have influenced what your grandmother did, and wasn't she your main contact with Faerie?"

"I suppose so."

I sent a desperate look to Basil, who frantically flipped through the papers in front of him.

The archivist turned around and addressed the jury. "I would like to rest on the fact that Queen Reine, if she even deserves the title, did not suffer during her exile, and in fact was quite careless with others' lives during it. She desperately wanted to return to Faerie, and her desperation led her to violate the laws around interference with human history. Witness the tragic end to this family, who suffered at several points along the way."

The jury murmured among themselves, and I turned to the judge. "Your Honor, may I say a few words on my own behalf?"

32

REINE

B asil, ever the gentleman, helped me down from the witness stand. I faced the courtroom and made sure my voice would carry.

"I would like to clear some things up. My leaving Aoine's was to keep from being involved in something I didn't feel comfortable with." I didn't think accusing her of treason would land well, so I kept it at that. "And maybe I didn't handle it well, but it had been a tough journey, mostly due to the interference from certain individuals who didn't want me to return to Faerie." I inclined my head toward my mother. "She was the one who convinced my grandmother to send us into exile, and while she supported me, she never did so to the point where I could gain enough allies to force my way back in. In fact, I did everything I could to not interact with people, but since humans are herd animals, they wouldn't allow it." I smiled, thinking of Selene's persistence in the face of my brusqueness and how Gabriel and Max had been there for me when I needed them.

"In fact, I helped many lives, many more than I inadvertently changed. In recent times, I cured a wizard who'd gotten in over his head with blood magic and a werewolf who had been burned by a Fae-fire bomb. The witch who was killed when I was in The Aerie had been feeding off its energy and keeping its inhabitants from procreating, which as I recall from the laws, is a death sentence."

The mood in the room lightened slightly, and I took the first full breath I'd gotten since I'd walked into the space. I continued, "As for my interference, I would like to argue that in addition to the education I received here about the other realms, I also studied what the inhabitants of the Earth Realm think of us. Have you ever heard of fairy tales? Or perhaps of a gentleman named William Shakespeare?" Now smiles and nods replaced stern expressions. "I haven't put anyone to sleep for a thousand years, changed anyone into a frog, or caused any trouble for any princesses except my mother."

A low chuckle made me smile at the youngest council member who sat on the jury.

"Obviously others have caused more chaos and damage to human lives than I have, and yet they are not on trial. I admit I have made mistakes, and I fully own that I acted inconsiderately in my singlemindedness to help my brother. But that's what the humans do—most of them will go to any length to help a family member. And I would like to point out that the Queen Spell skipped my mother and landed on me because she acted counter to that."

Basil made a swiping motion across his throat, so I stopped short of suggesting that she should be the one on trial.

"In order to tie up this final loose end before I can come and fully take on my throne as Queen of Faerie, and thus satisfy the bargain I foolishly made with my mother several Earth Realm months ago, I will use the remainder of my wealth in the Earth Realm to set up a fund to help the descendants of the original witch that Rhys and I got in trouble." And Irina and Meg, I added so the magic would accept that as well.

"Very well." The judge sounded less harsh. "The jury is dismissed for deliberation. The court is in recess until they return."

I returned to my seat on trembling legs and allowed my shoulders a centimeter of drop, but not much. Maeve didn't appear nearly as upset or frustrated as I thought she would. Indeed, she walked over to our table after the judge left and said, "May I speak to you, daughter? In private?"

"No." I crossed my arms.

"But I have something you need to see to believe."

Since the judge had left, I telepathically said to Basil, "*I knew she'd have at least one more trick up her sleeve. What do I do?*"

"She can come," Basil told my mother, "but as her counsel, I need to accompany her."

Maeve clapped her hands. "The more the merrier. And she'll need your advice."

We filed out of the courtroom.

MAEVE LED us through the palace to the dungeons. I hesitated before crossing the threshold.

"I need your word that you won't try to trap either of us."

"Oh, no, your decisions will be entirely your own. I promise."

Basil put his hand on my lower back, and I leaned into it to steady myself. I sent a prayer of gratitude to whichever god listened that although I had spurned his advances, he remained a friend.

She led us to the second level, and two guards nodded to her and stepped out of the way. She pulled a key from her robe and let us in.

The lone torch by the door did nothing to dispel the gloom, but I could make out three figures, each in a cell in the row to my left. I lifted the torch and brought it close to find Max Fortuna sitting in a catatonic state. His turquoise blue eyes stared straight ahead at nothing.

"What did you do to him?" I asked.

Her tone sounded too cheery for her words. "In this chamber, they are starved of their magic. If they can't access it, they'll go insane."

I walked to the next one, and the familiar contours of the figure inside made me drop the torch to clutch at and rattle the bars. Pain flooded out of my cracked heart and made me sob, "Lawrence! Gods, Lawrence, talk to me."

Basil handed me the torch, and I placed it through the bars so I could see Lawrence's face. Shallow breaths puffed between his blue lips. "Why did you bring him here? You are a monster."

"Oh, but you still haven't seen what's behind door number three."

I tore myself away from Lawrence's cell to find myself face-to-face with the half-changed Gabriel. He whimpered, and I could only imagine the agony as his magic fought through but held him in the most painful part of the transformation.

I wiped my eyes and forced myself to match Maeve's flippant tones. "You've convinced me you're a monster. But I'm still queen here, and I can release them."

"Go ahead and try." She dangled the keys in front of me. I went to grab them, then hissed.

"They're iron. How are you holding them?"

"Because she's not her," Basil said. "I thought there was something off about you. Who have you possessed?"

She laughed, and her form changed to that of Gerald Brigadine.

"Him!"

Basil groaned. "That means he's dead. She used the Dust and Ash spell. Clever."

Brigadine nodded. "And the guards out there are loyal to

Maeve. You didn't think you'd be able to completely eliminate sympathy for her here, did you?"

Anger burned through my fear. "What do you want?"

"You make a plea bargain." Now her voice spoke through Brigadine's thick lips, and his squashed nose made it sound more nasal. "And I let them go free."

"Let me speak to my counsel."

We walked into the hallway, and I had to stop myself from rubbing my chest. At least the ache meant Lawrence still lived, although for how much longer?

I swallowed my tears and turned to Basil. "I didn't do well with my last bargain with her. I need your advice. And please don't ask me to marry you or anything like that."

He inclined his head. "Don't worry, I can see who your heart belongs to. I can't give you the words but remember— make it as specific as possible and give yourself a loophole. I believe the letters we received were tampered with. I could feel there was information missing. Plus, she incapacitated two potential powerful character witnesses. Do what you need to buy us more time."

"And find Rhys."

He nodded. "And that."

We walked back in to find Maeve had forced the particles of Gerald's dust and ashes into her own form again. I should have recognized that she'd used such a spell, but I'd been focused on not allowing her to emotionally get to me.

"I will make a plea bargain based on a few conditions."

"You're not in the position to bargain here, Reine."

"Oh, but I am. How long do you think it will be before there's enough evidence to convict you of trying to kill the light queen of Faerie?"

She cocked her head. "Go on."

"First, you let them go and return them to their places of residence in the Earth realm. No tricks. Lawrence goes back to his house in Atlanta, and I get to call Barton Lucia to help him before we return to the courtroom. Gabriel and Max go back to their houses in Scotland." Selene and Lonna would know how to get help for them.

"All right, and what about you?"

"I will accept imprisonment, but not here." My intuition told me to ask for the last place I wanted to be, and I argued with it for a second before I blurted out, "The asylum in Cruaidh. It's been shut down, but it can be staffed again. I will accept imprisonment for ten Fae years or until sufficient evidence can be gathered that this trial was unfairly called."

"Make it a hundred Fae years."

"Twenty."

"Fifty."

"Thirty-five. That will be long enough that all my Earth Realm contacts will have passed on since time goes faster there."

She nodded. "Done." She snapped her fingers, and the three men in cells disappeared. We found ourselves back in the hallway outside of the courtroom. Maeve's form motioned to an old-fashioned telephone against the wall, which hadn't been there before.

I picked it up and dialed one for the country, then the cell phone number I'd memorized. "Barton? Hey, it's me, Reine. Lawrence needs you again. How soon can you get to Atlanta?"

I barely remember what he said, only that I managed to convey the urgency of the situation. Then I turned to Basil. "Can you explain it to him?"

He nodded, and I read both disappointment and resignation written on his face. Had I been a true queen, I would have figured out a cleverer way to get out of the predicament. Perhaps Maeve did have the better qualifications to be a Fae queen. She would have demonstrated her ruthless side and let the men in the cells die horrible, painful deaths.

Well, if being queen meant I had to be a cold-hearted bitch, then I didn't want the job. Had that, and not Lawrence, been the root of my resistance to it the whole time?

No, he still had a lot to do with it. And I'd find a way to see him again, although I didn't yet know how.

Now I recognized why I'd chosen the asylum—Fae didn't believe in therapy or mental health, so what need did they have for such a place? I'd requested the one site for my imprisonment that had the most human characteristics of any of the Fae structures. And my time in the Earth Realm had accomplished my grandmother's purpose for sending me there—I'd gotten a good education on humans and their ways.

Although the faces around me in the courtroom drooped and hardened in grim expressions when I accepted a plea bargain, I allowed my lips to curl into a small smile. And when the judge's gavel met the plate in an echoing *boom* that should have spelled my doom, I found worry, not triumph, in Maeve's eyes.

Good. Let her wonder if this time I'd tricked *her* into a Fae bargain.

33

LAWRENCE

I woke to find two faces I never expected leaning over me. The first was Barton Lucia, who watched the monitors at the side of my hospital bed. The second...

"Troubadour?" My voice sounded strange under the oxygen mask, even to me.

The devastatingly handsome blond Fae smiled. "It's Basil now, and good, you're back. Reine would've had my head if anything had happened to you."

"Where is she?" I lay in the hospital in The Aerie, but the mate bond still pulled taut and told me Reine was far away. I'd dreamed of a moment of relief, a spark of hope that kept me from giving up, and I'd felt her close by. What had happened?

"She's not here. She was about to win her trial, but her mother forced her into a plea bargain. Her imprisonment for your life as well as those of a wizard and a lycanthrope." He shook his head. "She kept strange company while she was in this realm. Including with this one. Doctor, can he take the mask off to talk?"

Barton looked at me, then at the oxygen and heart rate monitors. "For a few minutes only. I suspect he'll calm down once he gets some information. Even if it's not what he wants to hear."

I tore the mask off. "Dammit, I'm right here. Stop talking around me. And imprisonment? Where? I hope not in the hell-hole where we were."

"No, she's in the Fae asylum in Cruaidh. I'm sure my fellow dark Fae are looking after her well."

"For how long?"

His smile faded. "Longer than any of us would like. In fact, you'll be an old gargoyle by the time she gets out."

"Hades." If I'd been sitting, I would have deflated back against my pillows. "And I have something to tell her... Maeve commanded Rhys to shoot the dart that tranquilized me the final time."

Basil frowned. "He's been missing, but I doubt he's been working with Maeve. I'll add that to my list of things to look into."

I then blurted out something I'd never pictured myself saying. "This is a time for action, not research. We need to rescue her."

"Two more minutes," Barton said and left the room.

"He's a good sort, even if he is a Truth-Seeker." Basil leaned in and lowered his voice. "As for planning to rescue Reine, why do you think I'm here?"

ABOUT RISEN SHADOWS

~

Uh, oh, shenanigans are afoot! To find out what happens next, preorder *Risen Shadows, which will be released in March 2023.*

Ask your favorite bookstore to order it from Ingram Spark with ISBN 978-1-945074-73-8

A QUEEN IMPRISONED.

A reluctant prince.

A realm in peril...

The second dumbest thing I ever did was to make a Fae bargain with my mother. The dumbest thing was to make another one...

Trading my freedom for Lawrence's life seemed like a noble act, and if I wasn't already a celebrity in Faerie, I definitely am now. The problem is that being in the asylum means I have to play by its rules, and it soon shows itself to have a twisted mind and secrets to hide.

While I'm connecting the asylum's secrets to my past and the hidden history of Faerie, my gargoyle lover and mate Lawrence is dealing with political and family complications. I thought my mother was my greatest foe, but it turns out there's a bigger, deadlier game afoot, and Lawrence and I are the pawns.

Can I figure out how to leverage the power of the asylum to wriggle out of the bargain I made and claim my mate and destiny? Or will I be too late to defeat the voracious soul-sucking spirits amassing in Faerie and lose my sanity, my realm, my life... and my lover?

Sometimes even a Fae princess has to agree to an impossible bargain, and sometimes she has to break the rules. Guess which one I'm going to do?

RISEN SHADOWS *IS the sixth and final book in the fast-paced and thrilling Fae Files urban fantasy series. If you love snarky heroines, satisfying slow-burn romance, twisty plots, and stories that straddle mundane and fantasy realms, these are the book and series for you.*

PREORDER RISEN SHADOWS TO *finish this wild ride today!*

FROM THE AUTHOR

Thank you for reading *Shadows of the Past*! I hope you enjoyed it.

Do you want to keep up with the Fae Files and get access to special behind-the scenes info and previews? Join the Fae Files VIP newsletter at https://www.subscribepage.com/faefilesnews, and I'll send you the story of Reine and Rhys' exile from Faerie.

Also, reviews help me know what you liked about my books and help other readers find them. Please help me write more of what you love by leaving a review at the site where you bought the book. Thank you!

ABOUT THE AUTHOR

By day, clinical psychologist Cecilia Dominic helps people cure their insomnia. By night, this USA Today bestselling urban fantasy and steampunk author writes fiction that keeps her readers turning pages past bedtime. She prefers the term "versatile" to "conflicted" and has published both short story and novel-length fiction. She lives in Atlanta, Georgia, with her husband and the world's cutest cat.

ceciliadominic.com

Sign up for Cecilia's newsletter and get your copy of Perchance to Dream, a story that's only available to newsletter subscribers, at the following link:

https://www.subscribepage.com/CeciliaDominicbackofbook

If you'd like to get exclusive bonus scenes for The Fae Files, sign up for the Fae Team, the VIP list specifically for lovers of Reine and her world(s). Go to:
https://www.subscribepage.com/faefilesnews

I hate spam and promise to keep your email safe!

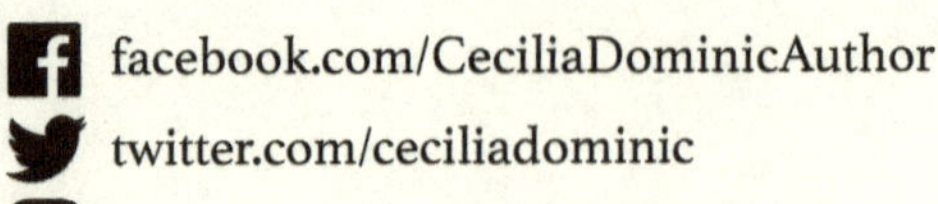

facebook.com/CeciliaDominicAuthor

twitter.com/ceciliadominic

instagram.com/randomoenophile

LOOK FOR THESE TITLES BY CECILIA DOMINIC:

Urban Fantasy Series:

The Lycanthropy Files
The Wolf's Shadow
Long Shadows
Blood's Shadow
A Million Shadows

The Fae Files
The Shadow Project
Shadows of the Heart
The Shadowed Path
Shadows of the Sky
Shadows of the Past
Risen Shadows (Spring 2023)

Dream Weavers & Truth Seekers
Perchance to Dream
Truth Seeker
Tangled Dreams

 Look for These Titles by Cecilia Dominic:

Web of Truth

Steampunk Series:

The Aether Psychics
Noble Secrets
Eros Element
Clockwork Phantom
Aether Spirit
Aether Rising

The Inspector Davidson Mysteries
The Art of Piracy
Mission: Nutcracker